Cameron

By
Angela Johnson

PublishAmerica
Baltimore

First printing

ISBN: 1-4137-1473-0
PUBLISHED BY PUBLISHAMERICA, LLLP
www.publishamerica.com
Baltimore

Printed in the United States of America

To my family and friends for their encouragement and support.

Part I

Chapter One

The clock read 2:07 when Gerard opened his eyes. The phone's annoying ring had awakened him from the most peaceful sleep he'd had in weeks. The soft voice on the line matched the woman he'd been dreaming about.

"Dr. Wright? Gerard, it's me Magdalene," she said through tears.

"What's wrong?" He propped himself up on an elbow.

"It's Cameron, he's missing. I went to the police but they didn't do anything. My husband…" Her voice trailed off and Gerard could hear her crying.

"I'll be right over," Gerard said and got out of bed. He put on the jeans and sweater he'd taken off a few hours before and hurried out to his car. He'd forgotten his jacket and this was one of the few cold nights of winter in New Orleans, but the urgency in Magdalene's voice made him drive on. Gerard had driven his housekeeper home on several occasions and had no trouble finding his way back to the depressed housing project. He had been meaning to talk to her about moving; he thought perhaps he had waited too long. A group of teenage boys in very baggy jeans watched him as he got out of his car in front of Magdalene's apartment. She opened the door before he even knocked.

"I was looking out the window," said Magdalene as she looked up at him. The wind blew her long wavy black hair away from her face.

"What happened to you?" Gerard frowned at her blackened eye as he reached out and lightly touched her face with its high cheekbones and smooth cappuccino-colored skin.

"They're going to steal your car."

"I'm not worried about my car. What's going—?"

"We're friends, right?" she interrupted him.

Gerard nodded.

"Will you take me to look for Cameron?"

"Of course. We'll talk in the car," Gerard said and led the way back outside. To his surprise, the car was just as he'd left it. They rode in silence for a few minutes. "You'll have to tell me which way to go."

"I don't know where he took him. He has some family down by the lake. Maybe..."

"We'll start there." Gerard turned onto the interstate. "Tell me what happened tonight." He waited, but there was no response. "You have to tell me. You know I care about you or you wouldn't have called me." Gerard paused. "I can help if I know what I'm dealing with."

"Leon wasn't always like this. Things were fine in the beginning. He played the piano at all the jazz clubs. That's where I met him. He was great, trying to get a record deal. He liked to have a good time and so did I. His family didn't have anything to do with him because of me, but he didn't care. We were happy. Then Cameron came and everything changed for me. I didn't want to go to parties anymore, but Leon did. He lost one job after another because of his drinking, and so did I. When he's drunk he's mean. I could take it. I figured he would get himself together soon and things would be good again. But he's only getting worse. I might let him hit me, but tonight when he came in he made a lot of noise and it woke Cameron up. He started slapping him for crying," Magdalene sobbed. "I started to fight him to stop him. He knocked me down. I must have hit my head or something. When I woke up, they were gone." She turned to face Gerard. "I called the police and when they finally came, they said there was nothing they could do. Then I called you."

She stopped talking as they exited the interstate and drove onto the quiet city street. Magdalene directed him through the lakefront neighborhood to the white A-frame house. Her husband's relatives hadn't seen Leon or Cameron in months, they said. They seemed more interested in looking them over than in a missing child.

And what a charming child he was. Gerard remembered the first time Cameron gained his full attention: Magdalene de la Valle had been working for him for three months since his last housekeeper had passed away. She was an excellent cook and kept the house extremely well, but Gerard had hired her on the spot without references because she was one of the most beautiful women he had ever seen. It did not bother him that she brought her child to work with her most days. They never disturbed him in his studio. He had seen a few scratches and bruises on her, but she never elaborated and he did not pry. One afternoon, he'd been trying, without success, to show one of the younger members of the orchestra how to play a difficult Beethoven passage. While they were standing in the doorway talking about when they could meet again, Cameron went past him and pulled himself up onto the piano bench with all the determination needed by someone so small. Gerard laughed and was about to call Magdalene to come get him, when Cameron began to play. Gerard wasn't sure, but he thought that Cameron played it better than he did himself. They were all shocked to learn that there was a little "musical genius" right under their noses.

"Well, that was very good Cameron. You heard me playing that just now?" Gerard didn't want to frighten him with his deep voice, so he spoke softly to the child and sat down on the piano bench beside him.

Cameron did not speak, only nodded his head as he looked into Gerard's intense dark eyes.

"Would you like me to teach you some other songs?" Gerard smiled. It was exciting to him to discover something new about music, even someone new playing it.

Cameron looked at him with his huge emerald eyes and nodded yes.

Now, Magdalene's voice startled him back to reality. He wiped a tear away from the corner of his eye. "Gerard, where should we look now?"

"Is Leon doing this to punish you?" he asked as he drove back towards the uptown area. The nearly deserted streets gave a false appearance of a peaceful night.

"I don't know. He's been …worse lately," she said quietly.

"Maybe he wouldn't head out of the city. Maybe he would go somewhere familiar to him, or to Cameron."

"He used to work as a tour guide through the garden district. He said it was his favorite place in the entire world."

"Let's start there," said Gerard and turned onto St. Charles Avenue.

They drove in silence past the historic homes and churches until Magdalene yelled, "Stop, pull over!"

Gerard obeyed even though he did not know what they were stopping for. A few moments later he knew. There was something lying in front of the huge ornate doors of St. Anthony's Church. Gerard felt sick as they ran up the steps towards the small, still figure.

"Oh no…no," said Magdalene as she scooped Cameron up into her arms. "Oh God," she cried.

"Let me see him. Please, Magdalene," Gerard begged. He wanted to check for a pulse, something. Bathed in moonlight, Cameron's complexion looked ghostly. He felt so cold when he touched his face that for a moment he thought there was no hope. But then he felt the faint heartbeat in his chest. "He's alive." He bent down next to Cameron's mouth. "He's breathing. Magdalene, let's get him to the hospital." When he looked at her again he could see that she was in shock. "Let's go. He'll be all right," Gerard said and when he ran down the steps with Cameron, Magdalene followed.

The bright lights of Charity Hospital were a welcome sight to Gerard a few minutes later. He had phoned a personal friend of his, Dr. Elliot James, and he agreed to meet them at the emergency room. Gerard gave all his information on the hospital forms and they did not have to wait long to be taken back. Magdalene was allowed to stay while they examined Cameron; Gerard was not. He waited, barely breathing himself, until they came out.

"I want to run some other tests," Elliot said. "He's in diabetic shock right now. We'll know more tomorrow." He looked at Magdalene. "I'll have to report all this. I'm sorry." He walked over to the desk and began making arrangements for Cameron's room. "You can stay tonight. I'll talk to you tomorrow."

"What all did he say?" Gerard asked after Elliot had left and they'd been shown down the white corridors to a private room in the children's ward. He looked at her grief-stricken face.

"He'll have to report to children's services that Cameron has been abused." Magdalene looked at the tiny boy lying in the hospital bed. She held his hand and kissed his forehead. There was a strange, distant tone in her voice that stopped Gerard from questioning her any further. It was too horrible to even consider, but in the back of his mind, he knew what Cameron's father had done.

It was three days later when Cameron was released from the hospital. He looked like his usual, beautiful self again to Gerard. He had come to pick up Cameron and Magdalene that morning. Cameron was excited to get the IV removed from his arm and could hardly be kept still. He climbed on Gerard's back and they were both laughing until the nurse came in with his insulin injection. Then the big tears began to fall from his emerald eyes. His mother raised his red shirt for the nurse, and she quickly gave him the shot in his abdomen. Cameron was still crying when the short ordeal was over. The nurse let him choose which piece of brightly colored candy he wanted and his tears stopped. He didn't happen to know the candy was sugar-free. Cameron fell asleep soon after they were in the car.

"Magdalene, why don't you and Cameron come and live with me?" Gerard asked quietly.

"Gerard, I…"

"I have plenty of room and it would be so much safer. Of course I understand that you only work for me. I would respect that."

A smile came to Magdalene's lips then. "We'd love to," she said. "Can you come pick us up this afternoon after I pack?"

"I have rehearsals today. I'll be back around 9," he said as he stopped the Mercedes in front of her place. "Will you be ready?"

"We sure will," she said and their eyes met for a moment.

"Ready for what, Mama?" Cameron asked from the back seat, startling them.

"I'll tell you inside. Come on," she said as she got Cameron out of the car. She and Cameron waved goodbye and as Gerard drove away, he realized that he felt something deep in his heart that he had not felt in a long time: happiness.

Rehearsals ran overtime and traffic was awful. It was almost 10 o'clock when Gerard turned the corner into the housing complex that night. He breathed a sigh of relief as he looked over at the graffiti-covered walls and trash-lined yards and knew he would never have to come there again. He saw lights flashing in the distance and as he got closer, saw an ambulance parked in front of Magdalene's apartment building. For a moment, Gerard told himself that there must be something wrong with one of her neighbors, but when he looked at her porch he knew that wasn't true. He started running towards Magdalene, who stood there in handcuffs with police officers on either side.

"What's going on?" Gerard asked the burly police officer who stopped him before he reached the steps.

"Sir, this is a crime scene. You'll have to leave the area." He let go of Gerard's arm, but stood in front of him so that Gerard could not get any closer to Magdalene than to see the blood on the front of her yellow dress. "What is your business here?"

"I'm Gerard Wright. She is my…housekeeper. What in the world has happened? Where is her little boy?"

"The boy is in the back of the squad car. There has been a homicide. A Mr. Leon de la Valle was stabbed to death in the kitchen about an hour ago. She says it was self-defense," said the officer, whose badge read "Caulfield."

"But..." Gerard's mind was racing. He looked at the police car and saw Cameron in the back seat crying and beating on the window. "You can't leave him out there. Can I go to him?"

"Sure. The child services worker isn't here yet," he said and led Gerard across the yard. Gerard could hear Cameron's sobs as Caulfield opened the door.

"Gerry," Cameron cried as he leapt into his arms.

"It's all right. Everything will be all right," he said and stroked the child's hair gently.

"I want Mama. Where's Mama going?" Cameron wailed as they placed Magdalene in the back seat of the second squad car.

"Cameron," said Gerard, as he tried to turn his head away from the scene and quiet him, to no avail. He was still trying to hold the increasingly hysterical boy when he heard a new voice over Cameron's cries.

"I'm Teresa Mason from Child Services. Would you like me to try?" she asked Gerard. He had not even noticed her arrive in all the commotion. He tried to return her smile.

"Cameron, please calm down. I'll take you to see your mama later," she said and wiped his face with a tissue she took from the pocket of her brown coat. "For now though, I'd like to take you with me to a safe place to spend the night and then tomorrow you can see your mama again." She gently took Cameron from Gerard's arms and into her own. "How does that sound?" She smiled a warm friendly smile.

"But I want to stay with Gerry," Cameron answered in his small voice. Gerard's mouth fell open for a moment. He had never spent much time with Cameron. When he was at the house, Magdalene did her best to keep Cameron out of his way. Now, he could hardly believe his ears.

"I can..." Gerard began as he looked from Cameron to Teresa.

"We have procedures in place. He'll have to go with me tonight. Tomorrow he can be released to family or, in some cases, to a court-appointed guardian. We'll know more tomorrow," Teresa said. "We better go while he's quiet."

"I'll see you tomorrow, Cameron." Gerard put on a smile. Cameron did not reciprocate. "Everything will be all right, I promise." He kissed him on the forehead. "Don't cry anymore."

"You'll come and get me in the morning?" Tears brimmed in Cameron's huge green eyes.

"Tomorrow we'll be together again, I promise," said Gerard as his voice broke. He did not try to speak again or the child would see that he was crying, too.

Teresa walked away with him and for the second time that day, Cameron waved goodbye to him. Gerard felt as if his heart were being torn out when he watched the car drive away. He asked Caulfield where they were taking Magdalene and if he would be able to speak with her.

Caulfield told him the precinct, but said no one would see her tonight.

Gerard walked away, thinking of his lawyer's phone number.

David Boudreau was in the middle of a campaign fundraiser when Gerard called him. He probably would not have come if he hadn't already collected the money for the $250-a-plate dinner. Sometimes knowing people could be very valuable, and everyone knew the prominent Boudreau family. David was able to get Gerard a few minutes in an interrogation room to talk to Magdalene. It was almost 1o'clock in the morning when Gerard and David sat down in the cold, gray room. Then the door opened and a policewoman escorted Magdalene inside. Gerard stared at the blood stains on her clingy yellow dress. She looked exhausted.

"Magdalene, this is David Boudreau. He's a lawyer. We want to help you." Gerard looked her in the eye.

"Gerard, let's get her story first. I only said I would come down here," David began. He untied the bow tie of his tuxedo. "Why don't you tell us exactly what happened."

"I thought it was finally over," Magdalene began softly. "I just wanted to protect my baby. I had packed the few things we had and we were sitting in the kitchen waiting for Gerard." She looked at him for a moment and then returned her gaze to the table. "Then I heard his footsteps. I know Leon's walk. I ran and hid Cameron under the bed in my room. I told Leon to get out, that I knew what he had done and that I would never let him touch Cameron again. His eyes were wild, crazy; it was like he didn't hear what I was saying. He tried to go in the bedroom, but I got in front of him. He pushed me out of the way. I got up and grabbed a knife out of the kitchen drawer. Just as he was looking under the bed, I stuck him. And he fell flat beside the bed. Cameron wasn't making a sound, but he saw the whole thing." Magdalene stopped, unable to continue.

"I'm so sorry." Gerard took her hand.

"Where is Cameron?" she asked.

"He had to go to protective services tonight. Tomorrow..." he began

"Gerard, let Cameron stay with you," said Magdalene. Gerard began to shake his head "no."

"Please, just until we find out what's going to happen. It would mean so much to me to know that he was safe, with you. There's nothing waiting for him at my house, or with my family. He would have a chance with—"

"Magdalene, I want to help, but..."

"Then help me," Magdalene's voice was strong, but Gerard saw the pleading look and desperation in her eyes.

"I can't. I don't know anything about children. I'm sorry. He's in a safe place."

"I know it's not your responsibility," Magdalene said without looking at him.

"Time's up," the officer said and Magdalene rose.

"I'll see you soon," Gerard said. "Hang on."

"I will," Magdalene said. Gerard watched the door close behind her.

"I can tell you're thinking about it," said David, as he walked with Gerard to the parking lot.

"Why can't we just take it one step at a time? You heard her story.

What do you think and, more importantly, will you take her case?" Gerard asked, raising one eyebrow. "Of course, I will pay for everything."

"This woman means something to you, Gerard?" David asked as he opened the door of his silver Jaguar.

"She's very special. She's never had a chance," Gerard said, as he felt his throat tightening again.

"I'll have to rearrange my schedule," said David, frowning. "But it's the least I can do for a friend." He smiled. "You've picked a strange time to grow a heart, Gerard. We'll talk tomorrow," he said before speeding away in his sports car.

Gerard stood there in the parking lot for moment, thinking. There had not been anyone who meant anything to him in his life in years. He was a self-described workaholic. He always said that he had not come to be the youngest conductor and creative director of the Louisiana Philharmonic Orchestra by devoting his time to his personal relationships. Music was his life. It was in all his early memories growing up in England. Even though his father had lost the family fortune, he had kept the title of "Lord" and, with his mother's money, they had managed to maintain the fiction of the English upper-class.

He had jumped at the chance to study at Juilliard. He and his wife, Elisabeth, had been happy there, for a little while. But Elisabeth was dead, so was their child, and Gerard had never wanted another relationship. He told himself that he had done enough damage already.

After Juilliard, there were several offers, but the least likely place had offered him the most creative freedom. It was too tempting to decline, so to New Orleans he had come. Along the way, he had plenty of friends, but nothing that really made any difference to him. Now he was crying over a woman he had never touched and thinking of taking in a child who was not his own. What in the world was he thinking? Gerard got into his black Mercedes and drove home.

Chapter Two

As he drove to the children's shelter the next morning, Gerard tried to convince himself that he had made the right decision. He had hardly slept at all and was parked in front of the building before it opened at 8 o'clock. The sound of crying infants met him as he went in the door and signed in.

"Are you here to see Cameron de la Valle?" A young woman in hospital scrubs walked over to him.

"Yes, I am." Gerard nodded.

"Come with me please," she said and led him down a long, dimly lit corridor. "I'm afraid Cameron is still in the medical ward. He may not be awake yet," she added as they went through swinging double doors and into what looked like a scaled-down version of an emergency room. Children were in short rows of hospital beds on either side of the room. "Everything doesn't require a trip to the hospital," she explained. "But, we may have to transfer Cameron. It depends on what the doctor says."

"Transfer him for what?" Gerard asked as they stopped in front of the bed in the corner. Then he looked down at Cameron. "What the hell is this?" Gerard asked and instinctively reached for one of the leather restraints.

"No sir, you can't remove those until the doctor says it's okay. He usually comes after 9."

"He's six years old. Why would you need these? Look at him, he's asleep." Gerard could feel himself losing control of his temper.

"We can't take them off. We only use them in extreme cases, anyway. We could not control him last night and we didn't want him to hurt himself."

"Get the doctor on the phone then, or better yet, find whoever I need to talk to about getting him out of here. This is ridiculous." Gerard spoke quietly in a concentrated effort to keep from shouting. He reached over and smoothed Cameron's hair. He unfastened the restraints. "You don't belong here," he whispered to the sleeping child. "I'm going to take you out of here."

There was a phone on the counter across from Cameron's room. He went out and called David. He could explain about "temporary guardianship."

After he got off the phone with Gerard, David dialed another number. Even though David had not called her in months, he still knew the number by heart. She answered on the fourth ring. "I was just about to give up," he said.

"Well, David…this is a surprise. I thought you already had given up on me."

"Of course not."

"I haven't heard from you in a long time. You didn't even return my phone calls. What's the special occasion?"

"I need a favor."

"I don't think so." Her voice was cold.

"Do you want to make some money then?" David had hoped his charm would be enough.

"You know I do." She smiled at herself in the mirror. Her bobbed haircut looked wonderful on her straight honey-blonde hair. She had adopted a new look for a new city. She had gotten into enough trouble in Atlanta to get kicked out of school and lose her job. David had been one of her best visiting customers and when she had come to New Orleans, she looked him up. He was nice, but she could tell that he had already gotten into something else. He introduced her to some friends and now she only had to work part time. Her wholesome college-girl looks were a big hit with customers.

"Do you like kids?"

"No." She laughed.

"Can you pretend to, at least?"

"Why?"

"I want you to get a job as a nanny. I know someone who will be looking for one today. You'd have to get there before he could call an agency."

"You're kidding. You're going to pay me to be a babysitter?"

"A little more than that. I need you to keep an eye on a kid and tell me what he talks about."

"What have you done?"

"Don't worry about it. Let's just say the kid is a witness, but he obviously doesn't want to remember, or he would have said something by now. You'll be there to make sure it stays that way."

"And how am I supposed to get this job when there's plenty of other—?"

"You look like my friend's wife, who died. He'll hire you just for that reason whether he realizes it or not. Make the little boy like you and you're in. Tell my friend you're a college student. You should ride the street car down St. Charles to his house. Buy a paper at that McDonald's on the way, like you have a full day of job hunting planned, but tell him I sent you. Just say you are a friend of my daughter and you two were here at the house when you mentioned that you were looking for a job. And I thought of him."

"I don't know, David."

"He'll buy it." He paused. "Come on Ava, I'll make it worth your time."

"You'll have to." Ava laughed. "I'll have to quit my night job."

It was almost two hours later when Gerard carried Cameron out of the center. He had never filled out so many forms in his life.

"Are we going to see Mama now?" Cameron asked in a small voice.

Gerard looked in his rearview mirror and saw Cameron sitting up in the backseat. "Oh, you're awake now. How are you feeling?"

"Okay. Are we—"

"Not just now. Are you hungry? We can get something to eat and then go back to my house."

"Okay," said Cameron and fell silent again. Gerard could feel those luminous green eyes studying him. He glanced in the mirror again and saw that he was right. Cameron seemed to relax when he saw him smile and he perked up even more when he saw the "golden arches."

"We can eat here?" Cameron asked.

"Sure." Gerard got out and opened Cameron's door. "Oh, I almost forgot your insulin."

"No," Cameron said and slid over to the far side of the back seat. "I don't want it."

"Cameron," Gerard said after he'd filled the syringe from the kit the nurse had prepared for him. "Come here."

"No, Gerry," he said and shook his head.

"Cameron, I have to give this to you," Gerard said and got into the backseat. He reached for Cameron, but he wriggled away from him. The closer Gerard got, the more he cried, and kicked. "Stop it," Gerard said firmly and pulled Cameron towards him.

"No, Gerry, no!" Cameron cried louder and struggled to get away from him. Gerard was intensely aware of how bad this scene would look to anyone watching. His heart was racing as he tried again and again to get the boy to be still for the shot. When his patience was at an end, he let go of Cameron abruptly and sat with the car door open, his feet on the ground, staring down at the pavement.

"I can't do this," he said softly and would have begun to cry like Cameron, if the petite blonde had not disturbed him.

"I couldn't help but see. I was inside eating. He's a diabetic, right?"

"Yes, and this is my first try at giving an injection." Gerard's face was flushed. He was used to giving orders and being obeyed, not reduced to tears by a six year old.

"My mom never gave me the chance to think about it. That's the way I do it myself now. My name is Ava. I'm sorry if I'm bothering you, but if you'd like me to try… ." She pushed her straight blonde hair behind her ear as she spoke.

"By all means, please," said Gerard, handing her the syringe.

Cameron had been quietly listening the whole time. Gerard expected round two to begin, but Cameron sat still and let Ava give him the injection.

"Unbelievable."

"Don't give him too long to worry about it." She placed the syringe back in the kit. "He'll get used to it." She smiled. "See you later, Cameron."

"Wait. How can I thank you?" Gerard locked the car doors and they walked in together.

"No thanks necessary." She sat back down to her coffee and classifieds. Cameron sat across from her.

"This isn't our booth Cameron," Gerard said, laughing.

"It's okay."

When Cameron and Gerard left the restaurant, Ava, their new housekeeper and nanny, was with them. She already had reference letters with her and was about to start another day of job hunting. They were all in luck.

It took the rest of the day to get Cameron settled in. After shopping and pizza, he was exhausted and asleep in the guest room by 9 o'clock that night. Gerard returned phone calls for a while to reassure everyone that he would be at work tomorrow and then went to bed himself.

The screaming woke him up two hours later. He jumped out of bed and raced towards the high-pitched sound that turned his blood cold. The light was on in Cameron's room and Ava was already trying to comfort him when Gerard got there a few seconds later.

Cameron was screaming, "No! Don't!" and when Gerard looked at him, he realized he was not even awake. He told Ava to let Cameron go; it seemed that the more she tried to hold him, the more violent he became. Cameron woke up a minute later. "Mama," he cried. "I want Mama.."

Ava and Gerard sat down on the bed.

"Cameron, you're all right." Gerard tried to reassure him. He hugged him for a moment. "You just had a nightmare."

"Daddy's coming." Cameron sobbed and clung to Gerard again.

"Cameron, you were dreaming. He's not coming." Gerard looked directly into his eyes. "I promise you he won't come back, Cameron. You're safe here." Gerard began to smile then. "Now that's enough crying. Why don't you sleep with Ava tonight?"

"Okay," Cameron said. Ava said she would take him downstairs for some milk and Cameron took her hand.

After they were gone, Gerard went back to his room, shaking his head. His heart rate had finally calmed down and he breathed a long sigh when his head touched his pillow again. Gerard left his door ajar so he would hear in case Cameron woke up again.

He jumped when he saw his door open a short while later. Light from the nightlight in the hall streamed into the room and Cameron appeared at his bedside.

"Can I sleep with you?"

"What's wrong? Where's Ava?" Gerard asked softly, as he moved over and pulled back his bedspread.

"She's asleep," Cameron said as he climbed into bed.

"Goodnight Cameron," Gerard said and covered him up.

"You won't leave, Gerry?" Cameron asked a moment later.

"I won't leave you Cameron, I promise. Now go to sleep."

"Goodnight Gerry."

When Gerard opened his eyes the next morning, Cameron was sleeping beside him. He answered the phone as soon as it rang so the child would not be awakened.

David Boudreau reminded him what time to meet him at court and that Leon de la Valle's funeral was that afternoon. He called it ironic. Gerard showered and dressed in one of the new black suits that his tailor had sent over. He combed back his jet black hair and put on his cufflinks as he went downstairs.

"Good morning Dr. Wright. You look wonderful," Ava said. She placed scrambled eggs on Cameron's plate. "Breakfast?"

"No. I'm in a hurry. You can call an agency and get some help, whatever you need. I want you to concentrate on Cameron, and your studies." He smiled as he poured himself a cup of steaming coffee.

"Can I come too?" Cameron was not eating. He was still wearing the Superman pajamas they'd bought the day before.

"No, I have to go to work today." Gerard pulled a chair next to his. "You'll have a good day with Ava and tomorrow we better find a school for you." He pushed Cameron's soft brown hair out of his eyes.

"But, I can play music, too. I want to go with you," Cameron said and began to cry.

"I'll take care of him. Go on before he gets worse," Ava said. Gerard thought about staying with him, but he needed to be in court for Magdalene.

"I'll call you. I'll be back by two to take him to the doctor."

It took less than an hour at court for Magdalene to be denied bail. Gerard was still thinking about how weary Magdalene looked standing there in a prisoner's uniform and handcuffs, when David came over to him.

"I'm going to try to make a deal for her. If I plead her down we can get this over with."

"You want to plead her guilty? It was self-defense."

"There were some irregularities at the crime scene. Maybe she killed him in self-defense, but not the way she said. It was not justifiable, so they say." David read over the report. "She'll have to stand trial for manslaughter."

"Manslaughter," Gerard frowned. "But if she pleads guilty, won't..."

"I'll ask for probation."

"Can I take Cameron to see her?"

"Visiting days are Tuesdays and Fridays from 10 until 12," said

David. "How do you like parenthood?"

"It's fine," Gerard looked at his watch. "I've got to go. I'll call you," he said as he hurried down the steps.

"What's the hurry?" David called from behind him.

"I've got a funeral to get to," Gerard answered as he headed for his black Mercedes.

Although he drove over the speed limit on the way to the chapel on 10th Street, he arrived at the end of the service. He joined the procession around to view the body. He supposed some kind of morbid curiosity was making him look into the casket. He had expected to be filled with rage when he saw him, but instead he was surprised that Leon de la Valle looked so innocent and peaceful. Then he remembered who he had seen asleep with that same expression: Cameron that morning. Gerard saw where the boy got his looks from and knew that he would grow up to look like his father. His pale skin, full lips, and thick brown hair past his shoulders made for a striking image that Gerard would never forget.

"Aren't you Gerard Wright?" asked the tall, thin young man. "You don't remember me, do you?"

"I'm afraid I don't."

"You judged a young musician's competition a few years ago. I won," He said.

"Alan Sullivan?" Gerard recognized the boyish grin. "What are you doing here?" He saw that they were holding up the line. "Let's talk outside."

"I put a jazz group together. Leon was our piano man," Alan said and lit a cigarette.

"That's where I've seen him before then. I came to hear you play one night."

"I remember," Alan exhaled smoke. "It looked like it might work for awhile. We were trying to get a record deal, and then Leon…lost it."

"How?" Gerard was intrigued.

"Leon was the best pianist I've ever heard, ever. But he always had problems. We just didn't know how bad. In the middle of our first tour, we had to take him to the hospital. First they said it was a nervous breakdown, then they said he was schizophrenic. Whatever it was, the group was over. I never have been able to put together a winner again. Last I heard of him before reading this in the paper was that he had gotten married to a real beauty. I guess that didn't do him any good either," Alan said with his southern drawl.

"No, I suppose it didn't," Gerard thought it was a small world.

Ava was waiting for him in the blue-tiled kitchen when Gerard returned from the symphony that night.

"You still up?" Gerard said from the hallway.

"I saved a plate for you," Ava said and opened the microwave. "Cameron is sleeping. You looked like you wanted to tell me something after you came from the doctor. You were in such a rush." She placed his dinner on the table and sat down beside him.

"I didn't want to talk in front of Cameron. The doctor said that he may suffer from some post-traumatic stress, or depression," Gerard said and sighed. "There's something else. His father was severely disturbed. There are some studies that suggest—"

"They think it may be hereditary?"

"She said we should be careful and watch him. A trauma this severe sometimes has lifelong side effects."

"I'm so sorry," Ava said, shaking her head.

"I understand if you…"

"I'll stay Dr. Wright," Ava said and placed her hand on top of his for a moment.

"I think we'll get a private tutor for him. Starting school is stressful, too." Gerard smiled. "I suppose we'll take it one day at a time."

"I'm sure everything will be fine. I better get to bed. Goodnight Dr. Wright."

"Call me Gerard please. Goodnight."

The medication the psychiatrist prescribed for Cameron did not seem to be working very well and they were all exhausted after another round of nightmares. They struggled through breakfast and were at the jail when visiting hours began. Gerard and Cameron waited patiently for their turn to go spend 15 minutes with Magdalene, separated by a glass partition.

"When can you come home, Mama?" Cameron asked as soon as he saw her.

"Soon," She looked at Gerard. "I knew you were coming, but I didn't want—"

"He needed to see you." Gerard tried to smile. "We've been getting along fine," he said and watched her mouth drop open.

"You changed your mind." Her eyes grew red.

"I couldn't seem to help myself," said Gerard as he looked over at the sweet little boy.

"Thank you," Magdalene choked out. "How has my precious boy been doing?"

"I miss you Mama," Cameron said and blinked. "What if Daddy comes back?"

"Cameron, Daddy won't come back. He won't." Magdalene looked directly into her son's eyes.

"He said he would," Cameron said quietly.

"No," said Magdalene. She almost reached for Cameron when he began to sob.

Gerard gave him the hug that she could not. His crying became louder and Gerard picked him up. "I got some medicine for him. Magdalene, David said there was something wrong at the scene," Gerard realized he wouldn't be able to speak freely. "We have to talk."

"I'll call you," Magdalene said just as the buzzer rang to signal their visit was over. "Cameron, Cameron," she said, trying to get his attention, but he was only growing more agitated. "I'll call and talk to you. It won't be long. Cameron, I love you," she said just before she was taken away.

Gerard carried Cameron to the car. He pulled over when Cameron started hyperventilating on the way back to the house. He phoned his friend, Dr. James, and he gave Gerard instructions on how to help Cameron through this anxiety attack. Dr. James even suggested that Cameron may need to be hospitalized for a complete evaluation. Gerard had heard that before, but his answer was still the same: "No."

When he got back to the house, he felt too guilty leaving Cameron with Ava when the child was still so upset. He phoned in again that he would only be there for the evening rehearsal. His secretary reminded him that there was no evening rehearsal because he was having a cocktail party for the orchestra board that evening.

"It won't be possible, Glenda. I have to—"

"I've already made all the arrangements. The caterers will be there this afternoon. It's not just the board. It's a lot of potential financial backers." She sighed and spoke to him as a friend. "You have to do this one. Everyone will be there."

"Thanks Glenda. I'll see you later," Gerard said and put the phone down. He sat on the sofa where Cameron lay. He was staring out the window as he cried silently. Gerard tried talking to him, but got no response.

After a few minutes Gerard went to the piano and began to play. Cameron turned to face him, but Gerard kept playing and in a matter of minutes, Cameron was sitting beside him on the piano bench watching his fingers.

Chopin's "Etude No. 3" had always been a favorite of Gerard's and he played through the whole piece from memory without looking at the music on his stand. He stopped and smiled. Then Cameron started to play. He expected a few measures before he would have to show him again, since Cameron was playing by ear, but to Gerard's amazement, Cameron played the whole thing, without missing a note. Gerard had flatted an E that should have been sharp, but Cameron played it correctly.

"How did you do that?" Gerard asked as he looked at Cameron. "Are you reading this music? But that's impossible," Gerard shook his head. "What note is this?" He pointed.

"E sharp," Cameron said.

"And this one?" Gerard thought it was a lucky guess.

"That's E, E, E, D, and C," Cameron began to read the sheet music.

"Who taught you to read music like this?"

"Daddy," Cameron looked down at the keys. "Before he got sick. Sometimes, music would make Daddy feel better, sometimes it didn't."

"Oh," Gerard wished that he hadn't brought it up. He had to change the subject. "Had you learned this music before?"

"When Mama was cooking, sometimes I would come in here and look at your music books. I'm sorry."

"Sorry? Don't be. Why this is…wonderful," Gerard stumbled and looked at Cameron, his eyes wide. "I've never seen anyone like you," he said and touched his hair. "Come on, let's go eat."

"Gerard, where have you been?" Charles asked as he tasted the caviar. "I came by your office to talk about the new budget, your salary included," said the chairman of the orchestra board as he laughed.

"I'm sorry, Charles," said Gerard. "There's been a lot going on here." He had changed into a grey suit and white turtleneck sweater and combed his curly black hair down smooth. He knew he looked the part of the maestro, but he certainly didn't feel in control. He just wished that this cocktail party was over and he could relax.

He was thinking of Cameron when he looked out the doorway and saw someone watching him from the top of the stairs. Cameron was sitting down looking through the banister. He smiled up at him and saw him get up. "I've got someone staying with me. Here he comes now," Gerard said. He was glad to introduce Cameron to some of his friends. Before Ava took him off to bed, Gerard could not resist showing off Cameron's remarkable talents. The Chopin was enough to get him an invitation to play a recital before the Christmas Eve concert. Cameron would be making his New Orleans debut on his seventh birthday.

The phone rang just after Gerard put Cameron to bed that night. "Gerard, its David. We need to talk. I've found out about some of the irregularities at the crime scene. We may have a problem."

"I'll come by tomorrow after work," Gerard said and hung up the phone with a frown.

Chapter Three

"Why in the world did you want to meet here?" Gerard asked as soon as he stepped onto the porch where David Boudreau was waiting. "I had hoped I would never have to see this place again." Gerard had been trying to forget the red brick housing project with its concrete floors and gray walls.

"Well, I certainly needed to see it. The police aren't gone. We just have to watch the tape," David said as he stepped over the yellow crime scene tape and went into Magdalene's apartment. Gerard followed him.

"I got a copy of the autopsy report yesterday. Leon de la Valle was not stabbed in self-defense," David said from the bedroom doorway as he looked down at the white chalk outline. His hair was wet from the rain and dripped on his Armani jacket.

"How can they possibly know that from an autopsy report?" Gerard sat down at the kitchen table. He was exhausted after the day he'd had. He wished there were two of him: one to do his job at the orchestra and one to take care of Cameron. The nightmares and panic attacks were bad enough, but the separation anxiety, as the psychiatrist called it, was the worst. He hated leaving Cameron alone.

"Because he was stabbed in the back first, not hard enough to kill him, though. He would have been dead in a couple of hours anyway from the poison he'd been given. There was heroin in his blood stream too, not a fatal dose. But the stabbing was the last thing and according to the ME's report he was laying down when he was stabbed in the chest. Gerard, that's not self-defense. Somebody went through a hell of a lot of trouble to kill him." He narrowed his pale blue eyes. "Do you understand what I'm telling you?"

"No." Gerard was glad he was sitting down because the room started to spin. "That can't be true." He thought of Magdalene and the blood-stained dress she had been wearing that night. Outside the rain pounded on the roof. Gerard looked up at the watermarked ceiling.

"Well, it is. Your girlfriend is lying. I asked her today if she wanted to change her story. She had nothing to add." David sighed. "Is there anything you wish to add? Did she confide in you?"

"I haven't talked to her since I took Cameron to visit." Gerard shook his head in disbelief. His black hair glistened from the rain. "Why would she lie?"

"You tell me, Gerard. You know I don't like surprises and this is just the kind of thing I don't need."

"Look David, I swear I don't know any more about it than what I've told you. That night at the jail was the first time I talked to her. Why—"

"I can only think of one reason," David interrupted. "She murdered him, maybe it was premeditated, or maybe it was revenge. Everyone knows how bad he treated her and the boy."

Gerard sat silent. He hadn't bothered to take off his trench coat when he ran inside out of the rain; now he was conscious of how cold he felt, inside. He had not taken a chance on caring for anyone in years and now the one he'd chosen—could she be lying to him? "What do we do now?"

"Well, they don't have the murder weapon. I could still try to work out a deal. I have some friends." David smiled. "Why don't you try talking to her?" He got up from the table. "It's late. We better go. But Gerard, she could be looking at some serious jail time if I can't work something out. You need to think about all this. Are you really going to want to keep the boy that long? I mean I can understand an infatuation," David said and put his hand on his shoulder. "But you're getting in over your head on this thing."

Gerard shrugged away from him. "I can handle it. Just do your job." He reeled in his anger. "I'm sorry. I'll talk to her tomorrow. I'll see what I can find out," Gerard said and ran through the rain to the black Mercedes.

"Is Cameron at school?" Magdalene asked through the glass partition.

"No, he hasn't been able to go to school since this whole thing started." Gerard took a deep breath to try to calm himself. "Magdalene, what's going on? How did Leon die?"

"What's wrong with Cameron?" Magdalene ignored his question.

"He wakes up at night screaming, crying, and saying that his daddy is coming back," said Gerard, his voice cold. "He has anxiety attacks when I leave the house." Gerard got louder. "He's on psychiatric medication that's not working well enough and I've gotten three different recommendations to put him in the hospital." He stopped for a moment and shook his head. "But I won't do that." He watched the tension ease in Magdalene's horrified face. "There's plenty wrong with Cameron, not the least of which is that he needs his mother."

"I didn't know it would be so bad for him," Magdalene cried. "If only he had a good home. I've never given him the kind of home he deserves, but all that was changing," she said, her large brown eyes filling with tears. "We were coming to live with you. I know he will be all right. I just know it."

"What happened?" Gerard waited but got no response. "Do you realize how long you could go to prison?" He shook his head in disbelief. "Is this your way of helping Cameron?"

Magdalene frowned and for a second, she looked at Gerard like he was a stranger. "Get out of here! You get out!" She leapt from her chair, knocking it over in the process and yelled at Gerard. "I would do anything for Cameron. You don't know anything about it," she screamed as the policewoman took her out. Gerard put on his coat and left.

"It's pointless. She got hysterical when I tried to ask about it," Gerard told David Boudreau from his office.

"You tried. I'll do my best for her. I'm talking with the DA tomorrow. I'll ask for probation." David paused. "So, do you want to meet at the club for a drink later?"

"I can't. I really ought to be at home with Cameron."

"Cameron? I suppose he is your favorite project isn't he? Your prized student. Well, I'll call you tomorrow and let you know about the deal." His voice was cold.

"Thanks David, and I am sorry." Gerard put the phone down for a minute, and then began looking through his pockets. He found the slip of paper with the phone number on it, in his overcoat pocket where he'd placed it at Leon's funeral. Alan Sullivan answered on the first ring.

"Hello. Alan?"

"Speaking. Who is this?"

"This is Gerard Wright," he said and heard some of the apprehension go out of Alan's voice. "I hope I haven't called at a bad time. I wanted to talk to you for a minute, about Leon."

"You want to talk to me about Leon?" asked Alan and laughed. "Why?"

"I probably should have told you before. His wife was my housekeeper. I know her and her son," Gerard said and wondered why Alan was silent.

"I thought it was just the music that brought you to the funeral. He played so great. Everyone should have gotten to hear him. His music came from his soul." Alan's voice grew warm. "That first year we were together, he must have written a hundred songs."

"What kind of things did he like to do? Besides music I mean." Gerard realized that the only way to find out how Leon de la Valle had died was to find out how he lived.

"Everyone knew Leon had problems. Sometimes he acted strange. He had quite a temper too." Alan laughed again.

"How did he show it?"

"He," Alan began. "Listen, I would love to talk, but I was expecting a call." Alan clammed up.

"Oh, I'm sorry. Perhaps some other time." Gerard could not mask his disappointment. "Alan, where did he like to spend his time?"

"Clubs mostly, especially the Jazz and Michelle's. He hung out there a lot. I've got to go."

"Thanks for talking Alan," Gerard said and put down the phone. He put Leon out of his mind for the rest of the afternoon and concentrated on his work. Rehearsals were in full swing as the orchestra prepared for opening night. Gerard arrived home as Ava was putting Cameron to bed.

" Gerry!" Cameron's face lit up. "Where were you? We already ate dinner," he said as Gerard hugged him for a moment. He breathed in the delicate scent of the baby shampoo Ava used to wash the boy's hair. His new blue pajamas matched his bedspread.

"I was at work. We have a new concert this weekend."

"Mine is next month. Ava showed me on the calendar that Thanksgiving is next week. Will Mama be home then?"

"No."

"Maybe for Christmas then," said Cameron as he looked at Gerard.

"We'll see." Gerard sincerely hoped that she would be there with them, if she wasn't still angry with him. He knew that he had hit a nerve at the jail, a very sensitive one. "What do you want for Christmas?" He hoped a change of subject would distract him.

"I don't know. You're going to get me something?" Cameron asked. He didn't know that the Christmas bonus that Gerard had given Magdalene last year had allowed her to put presents under their tree.

"Of course I am. Anything you want." Gerard found that this was the first time all day that he had relaxed and this was the best part of his day. He smiled at Cameron just as Ava walked in.

"I left dinner for you in the microwave, Dr. Wright. Is there anything else?"

"You've done more than enough. Please call me Gerard." He looked at her with his intense dark brown eyes. His heavy brow gave his face a serious expression even when he was relaxed. "Thank you for that. Thank you for everything you're doing."

"It's nothing." Ava looked away from his gaze. "Cameron, would you like me to read you a story?"

"I want Gerry to read." Cameron looked at him hopefully.

"Ava will read for awhile. I'll go eat dinner. If you're still awake when I'm finished, I'll read to you then."

"That sounds like a good idea," said Ava as she smiled at Gerard.

Cameron was still awake when Gerard went to the bedroom 45 minutes later after finishing off the penne pasta. He placed his glass of brandy on the bedside table and picked up the story where Ava left off. "The Prince and the Pauper." Gerard had not read this story since he was a child and found himself more interested in it than Cameron. He had finished the story when he realized that Cameron was asleep. He kissed him on the forehead and whispered, "No more bad dreams." He left on the lamp he'd bought for Cameron that projected stars onto the ceiling as a nightlight.

"He tried very hard to stay awake for you," Ava said as she opened her bedroom door and stepped out into the hall after Gerard knocked.

"I'm sure. He's finally asleep now. I hope it will be two nights in a row without nightmares. I'm going out for a little while. I'll be back later."

"Goodnight, Gerard."

Gerard drove to the nightclub in the French Quarter. The small sign and dark doorway gave no hint of the revelry of the crowd inside. Blues music crept out into the night as Gerard entered the tiny club. He took a seat at the bar and looked around the crowd of unfamiliar faces.

"How did I know I would see you here?" Startled, Gerard heard a voice near his ear.

"Alan." Gerard turned around to face the thin blonde-haired young man. "How are you?"

"Okay I guess." Alan sat down beside him. "What are you drinking?"

"Jack Daniels is fine," Gerard answered and a moment later, the bartender placed two whiskeys in front of them.

"Private Label," Alan said and sipped. "But then, you do look like you can pay for it." Alan grinned at him. "Drink up."

Gerard finished the excellent whiskey quicker than he'd meant to. His glass was filled again. "This is a little too good. I better slow down."

Alan raised an eyebrow. "So you want to know more about Leon?"

"Like I told you on the phone." Gerard took another drink.

"You've got the kid?" Alan finished his drink and ordered another.

"Yes, he's staying with me."

"Oh, I see." Alan looked around the bar. "I told you that I had kind of lost touch with Leon, but there are some other people here who knew him better." Alan pointed to a man sitting at a booth in the corner. There was a woman on either side of him. "That's Peter. He was our bassist. He and Leon hung out sometimes. The guy at that table over there was Leon's cousin. Come on, I'll introduce you."

Alan led the way over to the man with the dark brown, slicked back hair. He had very dark eyes framed by small, wire-rimmed glasses. Gerard could not help but notice the family resemblance and the massive diamond ring on his middle finger when he shook Gerard's hand. "Rob Pierre, this is Gerard Wright." Alan smiled coolly. "You two have some mutual acquaintances."

"Nice to meet you. Which ones?" Rob asked and gestured towards an empty chair where Gerard could sit down.

"Leon de la Valle." Gerard answered. His glass was empty and the waiter brought him another whiskey. “No thanks,” he said, sending it back.

A slow smile began to form on Rob’s face. “How would you know my cousin?” He shook his head.

“I never met him, but Magdalene was my housekeeper,” Gerard said, as he watched Alan walk away.

Rob studied Gerard’s face for a moment. “Is that all?” He flashed a smile of bright white teeth. “She is very beautiful isn’t she?”

“I’ve been trying to find out more about Leon.” Gerard had to let the question go by. “I just want to know— ”

“Why she did it? That’s easy, she finally had enough of him.” Rob drank more of his beer. “I told him if he didn’t stop treating her so bad, she was going to leave and take the kid, too. He would sober up and apologize and she would always let him come back. He’d stay straight for a while and then it would be the same old thing.”

“What thing?”

“Drugs, it was always something with Leon that he just could not leave alone,” Rob said, sighing. “I was starting to feel sorry for him. He owed people all over and it was just a matter of time before somebody put a stop to him. But then his luck started to change.”

“How did his luck change?” Gerard asked while Rob finished his beer.

“Everyone Leon owed money to got paid, even me.”

“Who paid you?”

“You don’t want to know much, do you?” Rob laughed. “A courier paid me. I didn’t care who it was anyway, as long as I got my money. Why do family members always think they can get credit?”

Gerard shrugged his shoulders. “I don’t know. Do you have any idea who was doing all this for him?”

“He must have found a new lover or something. He kept saying his money trouble was over. He wasn’t working and hadn’t sold any songs, so what else could it have been?” Rob paused. “Magdalene didn’t know everything Leon did. She thought she only had to worry about other women.”

“Oh, I see,” said Gerard. He frowned as he stood up to put his brown leather jacket back on over his red pullover sweater. "Thanks for your time. I better get going." He glanced at his watch. "I didn't see you at the funeral."

"I found out about it too late. Cheer up, she'll get self-defense right?"

"Right." Gerard said before making his way out of the warm club. The cold night air felt refreshing against his skin.

When he had parked the Mercedes in the back of the club, a street lamp had been on. He only noticed that the light was out and how dark the parking lot was now, as he began to back the car out. There had been a lot of people and activity near the club, but as he drove a block further down Dauphine Street, it got quiet and empty.

The speed limit through the narrow streets was 35, but Gerard slowed to 30 mph to be on the safe side. It was dark and he had not enjoyed so many shots of whiskey in a long time. He was starting to feel guilty about it already. Last year he had stopped taking the medication that the doctor had prescribed for him that made alcohol taste bad. The doctor had advised against it, but Gerard was sure he had a handle on his drinking now. He had been able to stop himself tonight, he thought as he drove slowly, and that was a great improvement. He was just about to reach for the radio button when he felt what he knew was a gun barrel touching the back of his head.

"Don't turn around. Just keep driving," a voice muttered. "You really shouldn't leave your car unlocked or a loaded gun in your glove compartment."

"What do you want?" Gerard asked, as he took his foot off the gas pedal and the car slowed.

"What do you know about Leon?"

"Nothing, nothing." Gerard said as he glanced in his rearview mirror at the ridiculous Halloween mask.

"Then stay out of it or you'll end up like he did."

Before Gerard could answer, he felt a sharp pain in the back of his head and everything went black. When he opened his eyes again the first thing he noticed was the blue lights flashing. Then he recognized the sound of someone speaking to him.

"Sir, can you step out of the car?" The police officer said at the door.

"Did you see him? Did he get away?"

"Did who get away?" The officer stepped back as Gerard got out of the car shakily.

"The guy who hit me."

"I didn't see anyone," he said as he looked at Gerard's eyes. "We got a call that a car had just run into a telephone pole. Where were you coming from?"

"A club a few blocks away," Gerard said, leaning against his car door.

"Have you been drinking tonight?"

"A couple of drinks," Gerard said and suddenly he knew where this was headed. "I'm not drunk."

"I need to see your license and registration."

Gerard reached in his wallet and handed him the license. "My car registration is in the glove compartment."

"Go ahead and get it." The policeman read the identification.

"I used to have a gun in my glove compartment, but the guy took it." Gerard explained before he pressed the button to open it. To his shock, the Smith and Wesson lay there where he always kept it. His mouth fell open.

"That's the gun he took?" The officer raised one eyebrow.

"Well, I thought…" Gerard knew that every word he said made him look worse.

"Step out. Wait right here." He brought back a plastic bag from the trunk of the patrol car. His partner was watching Gerard the whole time. "This is called a Breathalyzer test. You do have the right to refuse to take it, but then I will take you in on suspicion of DUI."

"I'm not drunk. I'll take the test." Gerard was confident this would all be over in a few minutes. Gerard did as instructed and first walked a straight line for Officer Davis. He felt things had gone well even after he breathed into the plastic tubing of the breath test. It made it even harder for him to hear when the policeman told him that his blood alcohol level was over the legal limit and he was under arrest.

"You can't be serious," Gerard said, shaking his head as he heard the policeman read him his rights. Ten minutes later he was handcuffed in the back of the patrol car on his way to the 5th precinct police station, charged with DUI.

Two hours after being booked and fingerprinted, Gerard got to make his phone call. His anger and frustration came through clearly when he had to leave a message on David's machine. This had to be the one night that he was out.

Gerard spent the rest of the night in a holding cell with dozens of other men who he would rather never meet again. No one was in a talkative mood. He sat on the floor, propped against the iron bars. He did not even get to give a message to Ava and Cameron. He was determined to stay awake to keep an eye on his cellmates, but to his dismay, he awoke to the sound of his name being called. He pulled himself up and began to dust the dirt off his black wool trousers. The guard led him back through the gray hallways to a counter where he gathered his personal belongings.

"Next time call a cab," said David, as he signed the last form.

"Don't start. Where the hell were you last night? I only got one phone call and I wasted it on you!" Gerard went straight to the exit.

"I went out," David said as they walked to the silver Porsche. "I guess you did want to have a drink last night after all," he added once they were inside the car.

"Just drive me home. I still have to go to the police impound to get my car." Gerard stopped . He rode silently until he knew he had control of his temper. "There was someone in my car last night. He pointed my own gun at my head and told me to stop asking about Leon. Then he hit me."

"Who was it?"

"I couldn't see his face. He had a mask on."

"This is sounding dangerous. The way I hear it, Leon was into drugs. There's no telling who all he owed money to." David sighed. "Maybe you should leave it alone. Let the police handle it."

"Maybe the police have the wrong person in jail."

"Not according to her. Look, I just don't want to see you get hurt. Besides, you have enough problems already."

" I was not drunk. I would never drive drunk." He had not felt so ashamed and embarrassed since he was a child. "I did have a problem before, but..."

"I've read the report. Your numbers were low. Things will be all right, but you're looking at probation for 6 months. That means no slip-ups, Gerard," David said as he turned into the circular driveway of Gerard's Victorian-style mansion, just off St. Charles Avenue.

"There won't be," Gerard said as they both looked at the brown sedan parked in front.

"Looks like you have company."

"Would you like to come in for coffee?" Gerard stepped out of the passenger side.

"I have a meeting, but I do have some good news. This wasn't how I planned to tell you, but the DA signed the plea agreement. They are going to recommend probation for this."

"David, that's wonderful. Thank you, for everything." Gerard smiled for the first time that morning.

"We're not out of the woods yet. The judge has to agree to it, but it looks pretty good right now," David said as the phone in his car began to ring.

"I'll let you go. Thanks again," Gerard said and shut the car door.

"Get some rest. You look like you need it. I'll be in touch." David drove away talking on the phone.

Gerard breathed a deep sigh as he stepped up onto the porch. He couldn't wait to get a bath and some sleep. He took out his key and was reaching for the lock as the door opened.

"Good morning, Dr. Wright." Teresa Mason said in an icy tone.

"Good morning." Gerard knew something was wrong as soon as he walked inside.

"This is one of those unscheduled visits I told you would

happen." Teresa did not bother with a false smile. "Are you in the habit of leaving a six-year-old child home alone?"

Chapter Four

"What are you talking about? Where's Ava?" Gerard looked past Teresa and did not see Cameron. "Where is—?"

"The front door was unlocked. When I came inside, I could hear Cameron crying. He's upstairs. I can't get him to come out." Teresa shook her head with a frown. "You better see for yourself," she said and went up the stairs ahead of Gerard. Cameron's door was open and Gerard expected to see him laying across the bed. The sounds of Cameron's cries however, were coming from underneath his bed.

"Cameron, it's me. What's happened?" Gerard got down on his knees and strained his neck to see Cameron at the far side of the bed.

"Where was everybody?" Cameron cried. "I was—"

"Please come out, precious," Gerard pleaded with him. "It's okay. Please Cameron." The boy finally began to move towards him. Gerard sat on the floor with Cameron and held him. "Don't cry. I'm here now. I'm sorry." He looked over at Teresa's disapproving face. "When was the last time you saw Ava?"

"When I went to bed last night." Cameron looked up at him. "I looked for you this morning, but you weren't in your room. Ava wasn't in hers either. Where were you, Gerry?"

"I...had to go out," Gerard stammered. He knew what the outcome would be if he said where he really was. "Come on, let's all go downstairs."

"I think I've heard just about enough, Dr. Wright." Teresa said from the hallway as she shook her head.

"I can't think what could have happened to his nanny. Something must be wrong. She would never leave him alone." Gerard stepped out of the den to talk to her. He could sense this was a conversation that Cameron might not need to hear.

"But she did." Teresa's expression was cold. "Do you realize that you could be cited for child endangerment for this?" She sighed. "I know that you meant well when…"

"Ms. Mason, things have been going pretty well. The nightmares don't come every night and he's eating better. His psychologist is pleased."

"I know that. I've already talked to her. I came over this morning to let you know that the case is up for review. It's your turn to let me know how things are going and I was also going to talk to Cameron. If I write this up, Cameron may have to leave."

Gerard's blood went cold. "Please don't do that," he said in a voice that was barely audible. "Give me a chance to find out what happened."

"He's a very special child," said Teresa, looking in the den at Cameron. "I understand that you describe him as having amazing musical talent, too. From what I saw upstairs, he's very attached to you." She turned her eyes back to Gerard. "You seem to have a way with him."

"I don't know what it is," Gerard was saying, when he heard the garage door open. A few moments later the gray Volvo he'd rented for Ava to use with Cameron, pulled in the driveway.

"Ava, where on earth have you been? Did something happen?" He asked as soon as she came in the house from the garage. He was alarmed by her puffy red eyes, and when he looked closer he noticed a red mark on her throat.

"I…Gerard, you're back." Ava jumped when she saw them all in the kitchen. "I had to go to the pharmacy to get Cameron some insulin." Her hands trembled slightly as she put her purse on the counter. She ran her fingers through her blonde hair. "He was sleeping and I knew he would need it before breakfast." Her eyes met Gerard's.

"Ms. Blanco, you should never leave a child his age alone." Teresa was stern. "Anything could have happened."

"I only left a few minutes ago. They weren't open yet and I had to wait, but I wasn't gone that long," she said emphatically.

"All right." Teresa looked from Ava to Gerard. "This is not my only surprise visit. I'll give you another opportunity, but if something like this happens again, it's over," she said and walked to the front door.

"Thank you," Gerard said as he shook her hand.

"Have a good day, Dr. Wright," Teresa said and finally smiled as she was leaving.

Cameron was not in the den when Gerard passed by the doorway. He had already moved on to his favorite chair at the kitchen table. "Ava's going to make us some apple pancakes."

"That sounds good." Gerard smiled at Cameron. "I'm going to get ready for work. Ava, I'd like to talk to you when you're finished."

"Yes, Gerard." She said without looking up from her pancake batter.

Gerard took the steps two at a time. He had a meeting with the orchestra scheduled for 10 o'clock. If he hurried, he could just make it. Half an hour later he had showered and changed out of the clothes he'd worn the night before. As he threw them in the hamper, he thought about burning them later in case they were a magnet for bad luck. What would Teresa Mason have said if she'd known that he spent the night in the jail? He was on his way to the music room to gather his notes, when he was met with the sounds of a Beethoven concerto. "Don't stop, Cameron that sounds great," he said and sat down on the piano bench.

"How was that?" Cameron asked after he finished the piece.

"It was beautiful. You've been practicing, too." Gerard patted him on the head and noticed his watch. "I've got to go."

"Can I go with you today?"

"Maybe next time..."

"But that's what you said last time." Cameron whined slightly.

"Your tutor is coming and..." Gerard began.

"Not on Fridays. Please Gerry."

That did it. Gerard could not refuse those emerald eyes. "Oh all right. Go get your jacket upstairs."

"Okay!" Cameron beamed as he ran out of the room.

Gerard took advantage of the moment to go into the kitchen. Ava sat at the table staring at her cup of black coffee. "Ava, is something wrong?"

"No." She looked up at him. "I'm sorry Gerard."

"I," he began, opening the refrigerator, "was sure there was plenty of insulin here." He pointed to the two bottles.

"That's what I just brought back. The other looked wrong, so I threw it away. I wanted to get it from the pharmacist personally…to be sure." She took a sip and tried to smile.

Gerard took a long look at the second woman in as many months to come to work for him with bruises and decided not to stay out it this time. "Ava, if you have a problem with someone, perhaps I can help." He looked at her throat. "I want to be your friend."

"Don't worry about me. I'm fine, but—" She stopped as soon as Cameron ran into the room.

"Ava, Gerry is taking me to work with him. I'm going to play with the orchestra."

"Not just yet," said Gerard. "I think I'll let you practice in a piano room with my assistant, Eric, while my meeting is in progress. Then we'll go to lunch."

"Pizza?"

"Whatever you want." Gerard put the insulin in his briefcase.

"You think you can handle it?" Ava grinned.

Gerard nodded. "You'll behave, won't you Cameron?"

"Yes Gerry. Let's go."

"I better call from the car. I'm going to be late for the meeting I called. Goodbye Ava. Enjoy your morning off." Gerard said as he and Cameron headed for the black Mercedes.

Ava sat at the table for a long time once the house was quiet. Then she took out the trash in the kitchen that contained the insulin she'd thrown away that morning while she was preparing breakfast. Cameron did not notice anything, but how many pancakes he received. She glanced at the refrigerator on her way upstairs. The medication that was there now was all right. Cameron was all right too, and she wanted him to stay that way. Ava went in her bathroom and took aspirin before she lay down across her bed. She wanted to go to sleep, but her mind drifted right back to the night before when the phone rang at 11:30.

"Hello."

"Ava, it's me. Can you meet me somewhere?"

"Okay, in the morning or afternoon?" Ava sat down on her bed.

"Tonight, it's important."

"David are you crazy? I never go anywhere and now I'm going out at midnight. Don't you think it might look a little odd?"

"I have a new idea. It won't wait until tomorrow. Can we meet at your place or my office?"

"I can't come out now. He's not here. I can't leave the boy alone."

"Surely the kid's asleep by now."

"He is, but…"

"Then come to my office. It's close and you'll be back before anyone misses you. If Gerard's there when you get back, make up something."

"That's easy for you to say." Ava sighed. "Okay, I'm on my way." She hung up the phone and headed for the door. Cameron was sound asleep when she passed his room. Twenty minutes later, she was in David's office watching him open his safe.

"I've got something for you."

"I've earned a bonus already? I haven't even reported anything. Not that a whole lot is happening." Ava sat down on the overstuffed Italian leather sofa.

"How is little Cameron?" David turned around with a small glass bottle labeled "Insulin."

"Well, at least the nightmares have stopped, for now. What are you doing with that? You're not diabetic."

"It's for you. You're going to give it to Cameron. I guess you haven't gotten to the other bottle I sent over. It cost me a bundle to bribe the pharmacy delivery guy. But there is always a way." David said.

"What are you talking about? What is it?"

"What does it matter? Just give it to him and it will look like he had a diabetic seizure. Then your services will no longer be required." He put the bottle in the pocket of her black leather blazer when she did not take it.

"But why, David?"

"That's my business. Just do this for me. There's $10,000 in it for you."

"No…no I won't do it." Ava frowned. "I'm not going to kill a child!"

"Oh, what is this? When did you grow a conscience?" David took a step toward her.

"What is wrong with you?" Ava backed away. "You are crazy. I'm going to tell Gerard everything."

"You're not going to tell him anything!" David grabbed at her and caught her throat. "You do what I said." He continued choking her, oblivious to her struggling. "I won't need you around if you're going to be a problem, too." He let go.

Ava doubled over and gasped for air. "David…"

"Are we clear?"

Ava nodded and ran out of the office. She locked her doors as soon as she got in the Volvo that Gerard had rented for her to do household errands. She felt in her pocket for the bottle. In the moonlight streaming through her car windshield, she examined it for a moment. She thought of David and decided she better drive home before he came out. She had never seen him like that. Nothing got him that upset. He was always so cool and confident about everything. He had never seemed to be prone to violence either, and now he wanted her to give a little boy an injection of something that was certainly not insulin. How could he even think her capable of that? How could he be capable of that himself?

When she returned to the house just before 1 in the morning,

Gerard had not come home yet. She was glad not to have to make up an excuse as to where she had been. David had left a bruise on her throat that she saw when she looked into the mirror in the hallway. She went into the kitchen and looked in the refrigerator. There was only one bottle of insulin left, the one she was going to give Cameron in the morning. Was this the one David sent? It looked fine, just like the one she took out of her pocket. The only way to be sure was to throw them both away. After she heard the glass clink together in the bottom of trash can, she walked slowly upstairs to her bedroom.

Ava spent a terrible night of bad dreams about David, and Cameron, and Gerard. When she woke up at 6:30 the next morning, Cameron was still sleeping. She redressed in her jeans, white blouse, and leather blazer and quietly left the house. She was surprised that Gerard had not come home at all, but he was a grown man, and it was none of her business if he wanted to stay out all night. Perhaps he had stayed out frequently before he took Cameron in. She drove to the pharmacy and waited for them to open. Everything went smoothly until she got back and they were all waiting for her.

Now, as she lay there at the edge of sleep, she wondered what she had gotten herself into. Although she had never considered going straight, she knew that she was no killer. What worried her most was that she did not know if David Boudreau was. She was not going to follow instructions and she had a sick feeling inside about what the consequences might be. Maybe she should tell Gerard, she thought, as she drifted off to sleep.

Cameron's presence caused quite a disturbance at the orchestra meeting. Before Gerard had a chance to send him to a practice room with his assistant, Eric, Cameron ran straight for the grand piano on the stage of the performance hall.

"Cameron, wait a minute." Gerard followed him.

"Gerry! Look at it!" Cameron stopped at the bench of the quarter million dollar Steinway. "I've never seen one like this. Can I play it?"

"Just for a minute. Then I have to go to the conference room for a meeting. Remember? Let me see where Eric is. You stay right here okay?"

"Okay." Cameron sat down on the piano bench and began to play the Beethoven piece he would play on Christmas Eve. Gerard listened as he walked out of the auditorium. In truth, Cameron's abilities almost frightened him. He had been practicing this music for only a week and already he had mastered it. It almost sounded like a recording when he went out to the hall. The music was so perfect. He pushed open the door to his office to find Eric Davis talking on his phone. He wrapped up his conversation quickly and got out of Gerard's plush leather chair.

"Sorry," Eric said. He smiled as he ran a hand through his black curly hair. He was tall and thin and his white sweater contrasted beautifully against his caramel skin.

"It's okay. Is everyone here?"

"Yes, they're waiting in the—what's that music?" Eric looked at Gerard.

"There's someone I want you to meet. Come with me." Gerard took Eric back towards the auditorium. To his surprise, Cameron was not alone anymore. Most of the orchestra members stood watching him.

"Dr. Wright, who is this? He's incredible," Eric asked once they were inside the auditorium.

"His name is Cameron. He's Magdalene's son. He's going to be staying with me for awhile."

"I read about Leon de la Valle in the paper. How's it going?"

"It looks as though everything will be fine." Gerard looked down at the floor.

"Oh, yeah, self-defense right?" Eric nodded his head just as the orchestra members began to applaud. Cameron smiled, but Gerard could tell that the crowd was making the child nervous, so he went over and stood beside him.

"I see you've met my good friend Cameron," Gerard said, patting him on the head softly. "That's part of what I wanted to talk to you about. We're going to have a special guest." He paused. "Eric would you mind showing Cameron around? Maybe he could even use one of the practice studios."

"Okay," Eric said. "Come on Cameron." He reached for Cameron's hand.

"No." Cameron pulled away. "I want to stay here with you." He looked up at Gerard.

"I just need to talk to everyone for a few minutes and then…" Gerard bent down to eye level with him.

"No." Cameron shook his head.

Gerard realized that Cameron was not going to let him out of his sight. Perhaps the trauma from this morning was still on his mind as well. "Wait for me then. Go find a place to sit." He spoke softly. He breathed a sigh of relief when Cameron walked out to a seat in the auditorium and sat quietly. Gerard watched out of the corner of his eye as Eric disappeared out the double doors and returned moments later with two cans of soda. Cameron was happy to get the unexpected treat.

"Dr. Wright, why exactly are we having this meeting?" asked Anna, one of the cellists. She laughed as she called Gerard's attention back to the group. They had made an impromptu meeting room out of the first rows of seats.

"I'm sorry. I am a little distracted." Gerard sat down on the edge of the stage across from them.

"He's adorable and he plays so beautifully," Anna said and smiled.

"A few nights ago at the party we asked Cameron to play a recital before our Christmas gala. I wanted to find out how everyone would feel about bringing him back at the end for our finale? I know it's making a change so close to the show, but…"

"I don't know," said Roger, the second chair violinist, shaking his head as he interrupted.

"Well, let's think about this for a minute, Roger," said Janette, the first violinist, taking over as she usually did. "This will be recorded and televised Christmas day, right?" She smiled. "Cute kids always draw an audience. It could be good for all of us. It's not like we could ever get too much public support."

"I think the saying goes, 'never work with kids or—" Roger began.

"I know. I know." Gerard laughed. "But how about just this once?"

"You're the boss," Roger said. "It's okay with me if it's okay with everyone else."

"Are you sure he can handle it?" Janette asked the question Gerard was not sure how to answer.

"Musically, I know he can," Gerard said and looked at her directly. "He's almost frightening, he's so good. I would love it if everyone else could hear what I've heard in my living room. It would be wonderful just to share music like that." He spoke from his heart. "I don't think he'll feel intimidated if all of us are there, too."

"You mean if you are?" Janette smiled. "It certainly seems like you've found a new protégé." She raised an eyebrow.

"The group is still my number one priority." Gerard smiled back to hide the fact that he was lying. In that instant, he knew that his "number one priority" was sitting quietly drinking a diet soda. He glanced out and found Cameron watching him, too.

A little less than an hour later, Gerard and Cameron were on their way to lunch. Gerard had promised that they could go wherever Cameron wanted. Nothing in his past experience had prepared him for the restaurant Cameron requested. Discovery Zone was a combination indoor playground, arcade, and pizza restaurant. The noise level was near deafening. He watched Cameron's mood change from quiet and dismal to complete exuberance as he headed straight for the huge pit of plastic balls. It made Gerard tired just watching Cameron jumping and running along with all the other children. He did not want to come out even when the food arrived. So they made a compromise: if Cameron would come out to eat, he could go back once he was finished. Gerard searched his pocket for an aspirin as they sat down to their pepperoni pizza. Cameron was so exhausted that he did not even put up a fuss about his insulin.

"I don't want you to overdo it, Cameron," said Gerard, pouring him the diet Sprite.

"I won't." Cameron took a bite.

Gerard shook his head because he knew it was futile to try and slow the child down. Lunch would be his rest period. "When we leave here…"

"I don't want to go yet," Cameron said, instantly alarmed.

"We don't have to leave yet. I told you I'd come watch you play some more. But later, why don't we go Christmas shopping?"

"Okay." Cameron did not look up.

"Don't you want to go pick out some toys?" Gerard had expected more of a response.

"I like toys, but I just want Mama to come home for Christmas Gerry. She will, won't she?"

"I think so, perhaps by Christmas. Do you want to go see her tomorrow?"

Cameron nodded. "I can tell her I played for the orchestra today."

"Would you like to play with them on Christmas Eve?"

"I already am Gerry." Cameron beamed.

"That's true, you're going to play just before the concert. But I was thinking, you could play with us again at the end, if you'd like to." Gerard was trying not to pressure Cameron. He had never worked with a child before and knew that he would have to be extra careful with this fragile virtuoso.

"Are you going to conduct me, Gerry, when I play by myself?"

"No." Gerard laughed. "I conduct the orchestra. I'm the glue that holds everything together. You don't need me for that." Gerard stopped laughing. "What's wrong?"

"But, I need you." Cameron's smile had disappeared.

"What if I sit in the front row?"

"No, sit with me." Cameron shook his head.

"I'll put my chair right next to the curtain. You'll be able to see me, but the audience won't. And then when you come back for the finale, we'll all be on stage together. Okay?" Gerard waited.

"Okay." Cameron slid out of the booth. "Can I go back and play now?"

"Sure." Gerard smiled and was surprised when Cameron hugged him. "What was that for?"

"Thank you for bringing me here. I asked Mama when I saw it on TV. She said we'd see." Cameron took off his shoes and handed them to Gerard.

"You're welcome Cameron." Gerard's throat was tight as he watched the boy run away and dive into the multi-colored plastic balls.

Chapter Five

It took several attempts before Gerard got Cameron to come out of the ball pit. He was about to have a tantrum himself by the time they left the noisy restaurant. Gerard ended up promising that they would come back in a week or two, with Magdalene. As Gerard drove towards the shopping mall, he couldn't help but think how nice that would be. He would take Magdalene on a shopping spree of her own. She certainly deserved one.

His head still hurt when he thought about getting hit the night before. Had it really been less than one day since he'd sat in the bar talking about Leon? Gerard glanced in the rearview mirror and saw Cameron fidgeting. "Leave the seat belt alone."

"It's too tight." Cameron frowned. Beads of perspiration glistened on his forehead. "I'm thirsty, Gerry."

"Cameron, we'll get something at the—" Gerard began speaking before he looked more closely at him. Oblivious to the car horns blaring, Gerard headed straight to the gas station on the opposite corner. "I'll be right back," he said as he stopped in front of the Circle K. He ran inside and bought orange juice. The clerk called after him when he did not wait for his change. Cameron was trying to lie down when Gerard got back to the car. "No, baby, sit up. Here drink this."

Cameron turned his head away. He was shaking. "No, don't like it."

"I know you don't like orange juice." He put the carton to his lips and began to turn it up, forcing Cameron to drink even though a little juice spilled on his jacket. "Here, drink some more. Come on, you have to." Gerard would not take no for an answer and finally

Cameron obeyed.

A minute later Cameron handed the carton back to Gerard. His eyes were as alert as usual and the trembling had subsided. "How do you feel now?"

"I'm okay." He blinked.

"You sure?" Gerard peered into his emerald eyes for a moment before putting his arms around him. "I'm sorry. I should have checked your blood sugar before we left Discovery Zone. You were over exerting yourself."

"I was what?"

Gerard smiled and tried again in simpler terms. "You were playing very hard for a long time." He smoothed the child's soft brown hair back into place. "I should have known better," he said softly.

"I had a good time."

"I'll have to do a better job managing your diabetes. I can't forget."

"I don't like the finger sticks anyway. It hurts."

"I know and I'm sorry. Maybe one day there'll be an easier way. Do you still want to go to the mall?"

Cameron nodded.

"You realize we're only looking today? No presents until Christmas."

"What about my birthday?"

"Well, I guess we'll have to let you open something on your birthday then." Gerard smiled and got back up front to drive.

Cameron held on to Gerard's hand as they crossed the busy parking lot at the mall. Some of the drivers had obviously mistaken it for a speedway.

Even through the crowds of people, Cameron spotted the toy store right away. As soon as they went inside, Cameron's face brightened. A deluxe electric train set was the first thing that caught his eye.

"Looks like an expensive Christmas for you, Gerard."

Gerard turned to find Alan Sullivan behind him. "Hello, this is a surprise."

"I was just out doing the mall thing and saw you two pass by. How's Cameron?" He asked as he ran his fingers through his blonde hair.

"Just fine. He's..." Gerard looked around for him. He spotted him near the front of the store looking at toys and motioned for him to come back. Cameron began to walk towards him, but stopped when he saw Alan. Gerard watched his face fill with panic. Instinctively, Gerard started towards him, but Cameron flew out of the store before he could get to him.

"Wait! Cameron, come back here!" Gerard yelled. He had to run faster than he'd expected just to keep the boy in sight in the crowded mall. "Cameron!" Gerard saw him trip and fall by the fountain. "What's wrong? Why are you running?" he asked as he picked him up.

"No! Let me go! I don't want to go back where he is!" Cameron struggled to free himself from Gerard's grasp. Gerard was aware of the curious onlookers and lightened his grip.

"I won't take you back to the store, but don't run away from me. You could get lost in here," said Gerard, softening his voice. "Okay?"

"Okay." Tears fell from his luminous green eyes. "I don't want anything. I just want to go home."

"Do you know Alan?" Gerard waited. "Have you seen him before?"

Cameron looked at the floor and nodded.

"He was a friend of your father's." Gerard hesitated. "Is that all?" He got down on one knee so they were eye to eye. "Did he hurt you?"

"I want to go home." Cameron looked afraid. "I want Mama." He said and began to cry loudly.

"I know." Gerard picked him up. "Let's go home then." He said softly. He looked for Alan on his way out, but did not see him anywhere. They were going to have to have a talk.

Cameron was silent on the ride home and the rest of the afternoon. Gerard tried to draw him out during dinner, but nothing worked. He was glad that Cameron's therapy appointment was in the morning. He went in to say goodnight after Ava had gotten him ready for bed.

"Gerry, do you think he'll tell Daddy where I am now?" Cameron whispered after Gerard had kissed him on the forehead.

"No, baby, I'm sure that he won't. Cameron, he's dead. He can't hurt you anymore. You understand that, right?"

Cameron looked at him, wide-eyed. "But he said he would come back for me later," he answered softly. "I heard him say it."

"Will you tell me what happened the night your father died?" Gerard could barely get up the nerve to ask the child the question that had been on his mind for weeks.

He already knew what had happened the night Cameron was abducted. The psychiatrist had played him a tape of Cameron's latest session. Gerard decided afterwards that he would never ask Cameron to talk about that horrible night again. Gerard felt sick inside just thinking about what he'd heard.

Leon was hearing voices. Cameron said how scared he was when his father "talked like he was different people, with a different voice and everything." It was some of these voices that had told Leon how to torture his son and how to obliterate a part of his innocence that should never have been lost. Gerard squeezed his eyes shut.

"Mama told me never to tell anyone." Cameron touched Gerard's cheek. "What's the matter Gerry?"

"Nothing." Gerard wiped the tear away. "You don't have to be afraid here, Cameron, and you can always tell me anything."

"No," said Cameron, shaking his head. "Mama said I would—" He stopped suddenly and stared down at his blue bedspread.

"It's all right. You don't have to tell me." Gerard did not want him upset again. He tried to smile. "Would you like for me to read?" There was no answer. "Something else then?"

"Well, could we go watch cartoons?"

"I don't think they're on."

"Ava tapes them for me so I can watch them any time."

"It is past your bedtime, but I guess one time won't hurt," Gerard said. "Come on. We'll go to the den for a little while." He watched the immediate happiness fill Cameron's face. He ran down the steps ahead of Gerard. They settled down in front of the TV. Gerard saw the light on in the kitchen and went to ask Ava if she would like to join them.

"I told you I won't do it," she hissed into the phone. Her back was turned when Gerard pushed open the door. He let the swing door close silently and heard the phone slam down a moment later as he walked back to the den to join Cameron. Whoever had left the red marks on Ava's neck obviously wanted a second chance, Gerard thought.

A week later, David Boudreau waited for his paralegal to go out to lunch. There in the piles of brown case files around her desk, he found the information he was looking for. There was always tons of paperwork with every case, some of it was useful and some not.

He went back in his office and sat at his desk to read about Magdalene's prior arrest record. Magdalene Pierre had been in a little trouble with the law before. When she was 17, she had been a drug courier. One of her deliveries turned into a stand-off with the police. Magdalene went to juvenile for six months. They believed her about the self-defense killing, but not about the drugs.

Of course, the judge in this present case would never allow the prior information in, but David knew he was the kind of man who would read a letter and remember when he was making decisions. Magdalene would not be getting away with probation for this now. David hoped the judge would insist on the maximum sentence. He smiled to himself as he looked out the window. He would have to leave by 4 to be sure his letter went out today.

David left the door of his Porsche open and stepped quickly onto the curb seven blocks from his office. He slipped the envelope in the mailbox and then got back in his car. He dialed a familiar number.

"Hello, may I speak to Gerard?" He asked even though he recognized the voice.

"Hello David. I was just thinking about you."

"Really?"

"About tomorrow. Are we to be in court at 9?"

"Yes." David hid his disappointment. "I see there was no need to remind you." He tried to laugh. "How is everything going?"

"Everything is okay. We're keeping busy with the concert coming up in a few days. I guess Magdalene will be coming home to us tomorrow, just in time for Christmas. I haven't told Cameron. He'll be so excited."

"Well, I'll see you at the courthouse then."

"Yes, I'll be there. Goodnight David."

"Goodnight Gerard," David said and hung up his mobile phone with a frown. He cursed Gerard silently for only ever thinking of Magdalene and that kid. When had he changed so much? Well, she was going to be out of the way after tomorrow, and he had another way to get rid of Cameron, too. Ava had been a surprise with her soft heart, but never mind now. Cameron would be away from Gerard and no one would have to get their hands dirty. He pushed the speed limit home to his mansion. He wanted to get plenty of rest. He knew he had a big day tomorrow.

Gerard opened his eyes and smiled. He had gone to bed alone, but Cameron had come in during the night again. The only time he looked completely peaceful was when he was sleeping. Gerard did not mind, though. If it made Cameron feel safer in between nightmares, it was fine with him. He got out of bed quietly and headed for the shower. He picked out a gray suit from his huge walk through closet on his way to the marble-tiled bathroom. When he came out dressed for court, he was surprised to see Cameron still sleeping. He looked back over his shoulder at him before he went down the stairs.

"Would you like some coffee?" Ava asked from the kitchen doorway.

"I don't really have time, but thanks."

"I was wondering..." She hesitated.

"Magdalene's release doesn't mean we won't need you here. You can stay on." Gerard knew what she wanted.

"Thank you. He'll be so happy to have his mother back," Ava said. "He's gotten very attached to you."

"As I have to him," Gerard said. "I'll see you later."

"Call me from court." Ava called after him.

Gerard arrived 30 minutes early and, after going through the security checks, found a seat on the third row. David came in a few minutes later. He took off his tan overcoat and handed it to his assistant.

"Good morning." Gerard walked over and shook his hand.

"Good morning." David smiled confidently. "Just hold on a little while longer. This will all be over in a few minutes."

"I'm looking forward to that." Gerard said as he returned to his seat and waited for court to begin. His heart skipped a beat when the bailiff said "All rise" a few minutes later. Magdalene looked nice in the navy blue long sleeved coatdress that he and Ava had picked for her the day before. Her face looked tired, but Gerard was planning to take her away on a long vacation after this was over. The charges were read and Magdalene pleaded guilty to manslaughter. The assistant D.A. made a sentence recommendation of probation and Gerard waited to hear the judge respond.

The white haired man read over the paper in front of him. "In reviewing the questionable circumstances in this case, I have decided to reject your recommendation." He looked at Magdalene. "Please rise. I sentence you to the maximum allowed for manslaughter and that is 20 years. However, you will remain eligible for parole..."

Gerard had stopped breathing for several moments when the judge began to speak. This was impossible. He looked at David who was focusing all his attention on the judge. He jumped up when he heard the gavel.

"Your Honor," David began to protest. The judge duly acknowledged his remarks and retired to his chambers. Court was adjourned.

Gerard walked down the long gray hall of the courthouse and opened the door to a tiny office, where Magdalene sat. It was the first time Gerard had not been separated from her by a glass partition in over a month. They embraced tightly.

"I don't know what happened."

"You did the best you could. They must have found out about before." Magdalene sat back down.

"Before what?"

"When I was 17, I almost got sent to juvenile for…"

"That's not supposed to count against you now," Gerard said, interrupting her. "We'll appeal this. David is talking to the District Attorney right now." The room grew silent. "Magdalene, I never expected this to happen. I don't know what to say." That was true. Gerard had been in shock since the verdict.

"I guess there's nothing to say."

Gerard took both her hands in his. "There is something to say. You know what it is, don't you?"

She looked at him with her beautiful warm brown eyes. "I don't want to say it. I did what I had to."

"You didn't kill him did you?" Gerard knew the answer already.

Magdalene shook her head. "I went next door to say goodbye to my friend Lisa. When I came back, Cameron was standing there beside Leon, with the knife in his hand. There was a little blood, but I knew he was dead." Her voice broke. "I couldn't let them take him away. I took the knife and stabbed him again." She was sobbing. "I wish I had done it myself. He's just a little boy. Leon deserved killing." Gerard held her in his arms as she cried, just the way he had held Cameron.

"Magdalene…"

"I'll never tell this to anyone else. You won't either, will you?"

"No." Gerard handed her his handkerchief. "I'll keep Cameron with me," he said and saw her eyes brighten. "You'll be out of this mess soon enough. We'll appeal this. It won't be long."

"Time's up. I have to take her back now," the red haired officer said.

"David will keep doing everything he can. It'll just be a little while longer," Gerard said as Magdalene held out her hands for the cuffs.

"Take care of my baby."

"Of course," Gerard managed to get out before he broke down. His eyes met Magdalene's for a moment before she was led away. Gerard tried to pull himself together before he left the room.

The desk clerk held out a yellow piece of paper to him when he walked out into the corridor. Gerard read the note from David and headed for the exit. The damp coldness of December dried the remainder of his tears as he went to his black Mercedes.

"Okay then. Thanks for returning my call," David said and put down the receiver of the phone on his huge mahogany desk. "Gerard, you got here sooner than I expected. They gave you a room to talk in, didn't they?"

"Yes, they did." Gerard closed the door behind him. "David, what happened? You said that she would get probation."

"Gerard, try to calm down." He got up from his desk. "Here, drink this."

"Thank you." Gerard took the whiskey.

"I am still trying to find out. I was just talking to a friend at the DA's office. Here is what we'll do. I'm going to file an appeal right away. We'll get a new trial and I'm sure we'll win."

"Do juvenile convictions count against you?"

"No, when you turn 18, you get a clean slate in our court system. Why?"

"Magdalene had a plea agreement when she was 17. Maybe the judge took that into consideration or..."

"No, all that is kept sealed for that very reason. The judge today wouldn't have that information." David took a drink from his glass. "Did Magdalene tell you about the drugs?"

"Well, yes. She told me that she almost got sent to juvenile."

"She was a courier for a local drug dealer. One night, someone tried to rob her and she shot him. The court agreed to give her probation if she gave names. She turned over some small timers." David did not realize that he was grinning. "Magdalene always has tried to play it smart." He caught himself and regained a somber expression.

"What happens now?"

"Magdalene will have to stay...incarcerated for the time being. Have you made arrangements about the child?"

"I told her that I would keep him."

"I don't know if that's such a good idea, Gerard." David sighed and swivelled in his leather chair. "I'm confident everything will work out in our favor, but I can't give you a timetable. Do you want to keep the child for that long?"

"His name is Cameron, and yes I do," Gerard said just as there was a knock at the door.

"The messenger is here with the papers for you to sign." Mary, his silver-haired secretary, smiled. "Would you like for me to bring them in or—"

"I'll come out." David finished for her. "Gerard, I'll be right back."

Gerard sat there alone in the luxurious office. He got up to pour himself another whiskey and felt a sensation of guilt as he poured. He knew that he was not supposed to drink alcohol. The silver coffee service sat at the end of the bar. That would be a better choice. Gerard looked around the office as he poured

David Boudreau's calendar was open on his desk and Gerard

glanced at it. There were the typical entries of court dates and tee times. Penciled in the corner at the bottom of the page was an address that Gerard knew he had seen somewhere before, but where? Gerard was standing there trying to remember the last time he'd been down by the lake when the office door opened again.

"I was just pouring myself a cup of coffee." Gerard explained as he backed away from the desk.

"I'm sorry, but this is going to take awhile." David looked at the spot where Gerard had been looking. "Perhaps I should call you at home?"

"Okay, that would be fine." Gerard did not meet his stare as he got his coat and prepared to leave.

"Take care, Gerard. I'll call you later," David called after him. Gerard walked slowly out to his car. He remembered the last time he'd been by the lake. The night he and Magdalene had searched for Cameron. He would have spent more time wondering why David had Leon's relatives' address, but there was a more urgent question on his mind. How would he ever be able to tell Cameron that his mother was not coming home?

Chapter Six

Gerard went to FAO Schwartz instead of straight home. There had to be something in the largest toy store in the city that would make one little boy happy. The shelves were filled with giant stuffed animals, building sets, and a few toys that Gerard had never even heard of.

"May I help you find something?" The sales clerk smiled warmly. She looked just young enough to truly appreciate a seasonal job like this one. She flipped her curly brown hair back out of her face.

"Do I look lost?" Gerard laughed. "I'm looking for something for a seven-year-old boy. It's his birthday tomorrow."

"Oh, a Christmas Eve baby. Does that mean that he gets twice as many gifts?"

"This year he will."

She was glad to show him some of the big ticket items, and Gerard finally settled on an elaborate electric train set. Cameron liked trains. The box was gigantic, but not too heavy. He placed it in the back seat of the Mercedes.

More dread filled him the closer he got to his home. But all his negative emotions disappeared as soon as he walked in the front door.

"Gerry's back!" Cameron ran to him smiling.

"Well, hello to you too." Gerard picked him up and hugged him. For a moment he looked into those emerald green eyes. So these were the eyes of a killer, he thought.

"What is it Gerry? Why are you looking at me like that?" Cameron asked as he put him down. "You were already gone when

I woke up. Where did you go?"

Gerard hesitated. This was not the time. "I had to go somewhere, and I've brought you a surprise. You and Ava wait in the den." Gerard looked at her worried face and she tried to smile. He brought in the giant box that had been gift wrapped with shiny red paper and bow.

"Wow!" Cameron leapt off the couch. "What is it?"

"It's for you." Gerard set the box down and knelt at eye-level with him. "Happy birthday, Cameron. I know your birthday is not until tomorrow, but you can open this one today,"Gerard said and watched him begin to tear the paper off. The look on Cameron's face was worth the $400 price tag. Gerard had already cleaned out the toy store at the mall in preparation for Christmas. He and Ava had hidden presents in every closet while Cameron was sleeping. As he looked at Cameron's happy face, he decided that he would not tell him about Magdalene until Christmas was over. That gave him two days to think of what he would say.

"Thank you Gerry." Cameron's hug startled him. "Can we put it together now?"

"Of course we can."

"I'll make some lunch." Ava looked at Gerard for a moment.

"That's a great idea." Gerard laughed. "I could work up quite an appetite here," he said as Cameron began to take the pieces out of the box. "Be careful." Gerard shook his head and sat down in the middle of the floor with Cameron.

It took almost an hour to put the train set together, but that was nothing compared to the hours of fun that Cameron had playing with it. Gerard had to plead with him to take a break for lunch. He fell asleep in front of the train set a little while later and Gerard went into the kitchen.

"What happened?" Ava put the book she was reading on the counter. "I thought you were going to call from court."

"I was so upset." Gerard breathed a deep sigh and decided that he would not tell Ava the whole story. She need not know about Cameron. "The judge rejected the plea agreement. He sentenced her to ten years."

"Ten years, for self-defense?"

"I don't know what happened. She had some trouble when she was 17, but that shouldn't have mattered now. David says he will appeal right away."

Ava glanced away. "What are you going to do now?"

"I don't know. We'll just have to wait, I guess. I don't know what to tell Cameron."

"He'll have to know the truth, as close to it as possible. Wait until after tomorrow or he may not want to play the concert."

"You're right. We have to get through today, and tomorrow." He smiled for a second. "Have you seen his suit?"

"That has got to be the tiniest tuxedo I have ever seen." Ava grinned at the thought. "And he does not like it at all."

"I know. I won't make him wear it today. Tomorrow will be trouble enough. I better go wake him so we won't miss the rehearsal."

"Gerard, I'm sorry. I'm sure things will work out."

Gerard nodded. "Thanks. Why don't you come with us? We'll go out for dinner after."

"Okay. I'll just go get ready." Ava smiled at him and looked into his eyes for several moments.

"Was there something else you wanted to say?"

"No, there's nothing else." Ava disappeared up the stairs.

Cameron looked like a little prince the next evening when he finally came grudgingly down the stairs. Gerard had the tuxedo made especially for him and it fit perfectly.

"I don't want to wear this, Gerry." Cameron took the jacket off.

"You look wonderful," said Gerard as he tried to comb his hair.

"Everyone in the orchestra will be wearing a tuxedo."

"Why?" Cameron went into the music room and sat down at the piano.

"Well," Gerard said. He couldn't think of a reason. "Because that's the way it's done. Please be still so I can just finish combing—" Gerard said as he ran the small comb through the soft brown waves. He was satisfied for the moment, but he knew that Cameron's hair would look different in an hour. His wavy hair had a will of its own, not unlike Cameron.

"I don't like it." He frowned and began to play Beethoven's "Für Elise."

Gerard could sense a rebellion coming. "When you're not on stage, you can take off the jacket and vest. Ava will hold them for you. Come on now, it's time to get ready to go."

Cameron did not move from the piano bench. "I don't want to go."

"Why not?" Gerard froze in the middle of tying his bow tie. He sat down on the sofa and did not let his panic show. "What's wrong?"

"I just don't want to." Cameron abruptly stopped playing and stared at the keys.

"It's almost 5 o'clock. Are you ready?" Ava looked elegant in her black velvet dress as she came into the room smiling.

"Not quite," Gerard said softly. "Why don't you want to go to the concert?"

Ava did not say another word. She sat down in the plush leather chair and looked from Gerard to Cameron. Gerard sat down beside him.

"It's too many people there. I saw them at the dress rehearsal yesterday and you said that was just a sample."

"But, I was just trying to tell you how proud I am of you. It just shows how special you are that so many people want to hear you play. They come because they like you."

"But, I don't..." Cameron began to cry.

"It's all right." Gerard hugged and soothed him.

"It can't be as bad as all that." Ava came over and stroked his hair.

"Gerard will be right there."

"Cameron, I have an idea. What if I'm your page turner tonight? I could sit with you." Gerard listened as the crying subsided.

"You promise you won't leave me out there by myself?" Cameron blinked.

"Of course I promise. Do you still want to come back and play with the group? Because I would have to conduct then."

"Well, I guess it would be all right if everybody was there." Cameron finally smiled and his emerald eyes sparkled. "Okay."

Gerard sighed. "Thank you. We better get going or we're going to miss the whole thing, anyway." He smiled at Ava after Cameron left the room to get his coat. "That was a close one."

The Orpheum Theater was filled to standing-room-only capacity. The video crew set up different cameras throughout the crowd to catch every angle.

"This is wonderful. I see lots of potential financial backers here tonight," said Glenda as she hugged him.

"You are a very smart woman, and you look lovely too. How festive." Gerard complimented her green dress.

"Thank you. I better get to my seat. It's almost time. Good luck tonight."

"Thank you." Gerard nodded and looked around for Cameron, who was sitting quietly with Ava in the front row. He motioned for him to come to him at the side of the stage. "Are you ready?"

Cameron nodded, but there was a flicker of fear behind his eyes.

"Just play like you do when we're at home. You make such beautiful music that I wanted people to have a chance to hear you. You have nothing to be afraid of," Gerard said and kissed him on the forehead. "You go to the piano and I'll introduce you." Gerard waited for Cameron to sit down before he motioned the lighting technician to darken the theater to signal the beginning of the performance.

"Ladies and Gentlemen, I'd like to thank you for coming tonight. We've put a tremendous amount of effort into the program tonight. This evening is a team effort and I'd like to thank all the staff and volunteers who made this possible." He paused for the applause.

"Recently, I've made a musical discovery. No, it's not a lost work of Mozart's, but it is rather amazing." He smiled. "I could explain further, but instead, allow me to introduce you to Mr. Cameron de la Valle."

The opening notes of "God Rest Ye Merry Gentlemen" instantly drew the crowd in and when Cameron moved on to the Handel pieces, they were completely spellbound. Cameron may have been dwarfed by the size of the grand piano, but his music was not. It was almost unbelievable that a small child could produce such magnificent sound. Gerard was more nervous than usual and missed a page turn of the music, but his seven-year-old protégé made it fine without him. The child had a half a page ahead memorized.

Gerard was astonished as usual when the recital ended 35 minutes later. Cameron had played brilliantly and the audience was on their feet for a standing ovation. Gerard gave Cameron a big hug and patted his head.

"How was that?" the small voice asked over the thunderous applause.

"You were wonderful, Cameron, I'm so proud of you," said Gerard. He looked into his happy face. "You were absolutely perfect. This is all for you."

Cameron walked to the center of the stage and bowed. Then he rushed off behind the curtain. Gerard waited at his podium for the orchestra to come out and he knew that Cameron was going to be a tough act to follow.

"Gerard, you were brilliant!" Glenda came over to him smiling after the concert. "This is Robert Goodman. He asked for an introduction." She whispered in his ear after giving him a kiss on the cheek.

"Good evening. That was a wonderful concert," said the short, dark-haired man. "I know you don't have a lot of time to talk right now, but I'm from Enterprise Records and I'd like to talk to you."

"I am sorry, but the orchestra already has an arrangement with a local company."

"Actually, I was talking about your little protégé."

"Cameron?" Gerard was surprised.

"Yes, I'm really impressed with him. I know tonight was his debut, but he was magnificent. I'd like to record him one day, maybe after he wins a prize. It's always easier to structure a deal after a competition. I'm assuming that we'll see him at the New York Young Pianists Competition in April?"

"I haven't decided."

"Well, here's my card. If you decide to bring him, call me while you're in town and we'll talk about it some more. There's definitely money to be made." He looked down and smiled warmly. "Hello there."

Gerard did not realize that Cameron had come and stood beside him. He did not want to talk to Cameron about any of this right now.

"Hello." Cameron said shyly. "Gerry, can I have some of that cake?"

"I don't ..." Gerard began and watched Cameron's smile fade.

"Ava said no, but she said I could ask you."

"We'll have to get you your insulin first, and only a small piece." Gerard turned back to Robert. "I better go with him. Thank you for coming tonight, it was nice meeting you." He shook his hand.

"I hope to hear from you again soon." Robert smiled as he walked away.

"Who was that Gerry?"

"He's a businessman from New York who liked your playing very much." said Gerard. "Now let's go see about that cake."

"Okay, and then can we go home?"

"Already?"

"I kind of don't feel good."

"What's the matter?" Gerard instinctively put his hand across his forehead. "You are a little warm. We can go now."

"But I want some cake. My head just hurts a little."

"Precious," Gerard began, but he realized that to a child, the cake was the most important thing. "Alright. Let's get the cake first."

"Gerard, we were just coming back to congratulate you," said David Boudreau. He and his wife, Susan, intercepted them before they could reach the dessert buffet.

"Thank you."

"How exciting, you've discovered a little prodigy." Susan winked at him with her blue eyes. She had darkened her beautiful red hair since Gerard had seen her last. "How long have you been playing the piano?" She smiled down at Cameron.

"I..." Cameron began with a shrug. He looked like he was about to say more, but his green eyes closed abruptly and he fell to the floor, unconscious.

"Cameron! Cameron!" Gerard lifted the child's head.

"What happened?" Ava ran over and knelt beside them.

"I don't know. He was fine and then..."

"David, call an ambulance." Susan waited while he took out his phone.

"Never mind, I'll drive him." Gerard picked him up. "Ava, bring his coat." As soon as they were in the car, Gerard turned on the caution lights and they sped out of the garage and down Canal to the hospital.

"Dr. Wright?" A young man with dark brown hair and a moustache came into the waiting room where Gerard and Ava had been sitting for half an hour.

"Yes." Gerard stood up.

"I'm Dr. O'Connor. I was just in with your son." He looked down at the chart in his hands.

"I'm his guardian. What happened?"

"He's awake now. His blood sugar may have dropped too low. It can happen, especially in children with diabetes. Right now, his most discomfort is from the migraine."

"Migraine?"

"We've given him something for the nausea and a pain reliever. He can go home, but he'll need quiet and dark."

"I didn't know he had migraine headaches. He's only six; I mean seven as of today."

"They often occur in children, but they can be managed. He told me about the concert. A big event like that could trigger a headache."

"Can I see him now?"

"Sure, I'll get the papers signed for his release. You should take him to your family doctor in the next few days."

"Thank you so much." Gerard said and shook his hand. He and Ava followed him back behind the yellow curtain. The tiny boy looked lost in the enormous hospital bed. They had turned off the fluorescent light directly overhead to comfort him. He blinked at Gerard. "Hi there." Gerard went to him and gently smoothed his hair as he spoke. "I'm going to take you home now. You'll be feeling much better tomorrow."

"Tomorrow is Christmas." Cameron looked away. "Is Mama coming home then?"

"We'll talk about it later. Come on, let's get you home."

Cameron slept all the way home and well into the night. Gerard sat beside his bed in the dark room. He did not want him to awaken alone in the dark. He had hours to think about what he would say to him, but he still jumped when he heard a small voice say, "Gerry?"

"Yes, I'm here Cameron. How are you feeling?"

"My head stopped hurting." Cameron sat up. "Mostly."

"The doctor said quiet and rest until tomorrow." Gerard sat down on the edge of the bed. "Are you hungry?"

Cameron nodded and sat up again. He did not complain when Gerard gave him his insulin injection.

"Ava brought this up for you a little while ago." Gerard reached for the tray beside the lamp on the dresser. The soft lamplight poured across the room. Cameron looked at the ham sandwich, chips, and pickle he had placed in front of him.

"Gerry, is Mama coming back in the morning?" Cameron asked as he crunched on the pickle.

Gerard looked into the child's eyes. "No, Cameron, she's not."

"But..."

"Remember when I told you she had to have a court case so the judge could say it was okay for her to come home? Well, it's going to be a little while before she has her court date." Gerard was thinking of the appeal.

"When?" Cameron's eyes filled with tears.

"I don't know exactly, maybe a few months. I hope it will be soon." Gerard sat beside him and put his arm around him. "It's going to be all right. We'll still talk to her on the phone every day, and we will go and see her." He didn't realize that he was crying, too. "Wouldn't you like to keep living here with me?"

Cameron nodded and hugged him. "I love you, Gerry."

Gerard was surprised at how deeply the words affected him. He hadn't let himself feel deeply for anyone in a long time, but all that had changed now. "I love you, too." He kissed him on the forehead and wiped Cameron's tears away. "We're going to be all right. You can trust me."

"I know Gerry."

"Now finish your dinner and I'll read to you for awhile if you like. In the morning, we'll open the presents." He saw Cameron begin to smile.

Christmas morning was usually a joyous occasion but this year Gerard had gone out of his way to make it special for Cameron. The historic Victorian mansion had been transformed into a child's fantasy of Christmas. He had spared no expense on decorative garland, ribbons, and wreaths. There were half a dozen fruit baskets throughout the house, but the focal point of attention was the eight-foot Christmas tree. He and Ava had spent hours decorating it, and on Christmas Eve after Cameron had finally gone to sleep, he went to every hiding place in the house and took out all the presents. By the time he got through placing them under and around the tree, there was hardly room to get close to it.

The tranquilizers that he gave Cameron every night before bed kept him sleeping deeply until Gerard woke him at 9:30. Ava was waiting downstairs with the instant camera when they came into the living room to capture Cameron's expression on film. Gerard got a gift better than he had even imagined when he saw the look of astonished joy on Cameron's face.

"Wow! Gerry, look at everything!" Cameron squealed with delight and ran over to a stack of boxes.

"Slow down. You have to read the names on them first." Gerard placed a box in front of him and as soon as he read his name he began to tear the wrapping paper. Gerard stood back for a moment and smiled.

"Would you like some coffee?" Ava asked.

"That would be nice." When she returned from the kitchen with the tray he took a silver wrapped box from his pocket. "This is for you."

"Gerard, I wasn't expecting anything else. That generous bonus…"

"I wanted you to have it. You deserve something special. You have been so helpful. I don't know what I would have done without you."

"Thank you." Ava took the box and looked away for a moment to keep Gerard from seeing the guilt in her eyes. It was too late to tell him why she had actually come there, and she never wanted him to find out.

"Oh Gerard!" Her jaw dropped when she saw the diamond pendant. "It's beautiful. Thank you so much." She hugged him just as the phone rang.

Gerard answered and listened to the usual prerecorded message. "Hello Magdalene." He said a few moments later.

"Merry Christmas. How is he doing?"

"He's doing fine. Hold on." Gerard handed the phone to Cameron. "It's for you."

"Mama?" Cameron said into the phone.

"Merry Christmas Cameron. How is my little angel today?"

"I got all these presents, Mama. I haven't opened them all yet."

"That's wonderful baby." Magdalene's voice broke.

"Mama, I miss you. I got you a present. Gerry helped me pick it out."

"Tell her we'll be over to see her this afternoon. You can give it to her then."

"I'll see you this afternoon then. I love you Cameron." Magdalene tried not to sound depressed. "I have to go now. Other people are waiting to use the phone. I'll see you later. I love you."

"I love you too Mama," Cameron said. He sat quietly holding the phone.

"Why don't we open the rest of the presents now?" Gerard put the phone back on the base.

"Gerry, I have a present for you," Cameron said. "Sit here, and close your eyes."

"What? Okay." He waited patiently in the recliner. A few moments later he heard the opening passage of Liszt's Liebestraum. His eyes opened automatically, but he was so shocked he didn't get up from his chair. He recognized the music as some of the most difficult piano music ever written, and yet he was hearing it without mistakes. "When—how did you learn that?" he stammered.

"I found it on your desk. I thought it was for me," Cameron said proudly. "Are you surprised?" He came over and hugged him.

"Yes." Gerard said and laughed. "It was supposed to be a challenge for you. Thank you Cameron. That was a wonderful Christmas gift."

"You're welcome. Gerry, can I open that big box now?"

"Of course. I'll help you." Gerard watched Cameron begin tearing the wrapping paper off the giant teddy bear and thought of Magdalene. He knew if she were there, the day would be truly perfect for Cameron, but since she could not be present, he was going to do everything he could to make the boy happy. And not just on Christmas, but every day.

Chapter Seven

"Good morning, Dr. Wright." Teresa Mason smiled at him from the front porch.

"Good morning. I was just about to call you." Gerard opened the door wide. "Come in. Did you have a good Christmas?"

"It was nice, thank you." She stepped inside the warm hallway and unbuttoned her coat. "How have you been?"

"Just fine." Gerard took her coat and hung it on a hook in the hall closet. He was not surprised to see Cameron standing in the doorway looking up at Teresa when he turned around.

"Hi."

"Hello Cameron." Teresa hugged him like an old friend. "How are you doing today?"

"Fine," he said and smiled.

"Did you have a nice holiday?"

He nodded. "Do you want to see what I got?" Cameron took her hand and led her down the hall.

"Would you like some coffee?" Gerard asked as he brought in the coffee service.

"Thank you."

"We all went to the Christmas light display in the park and took the walking tour. Ava has caught a bad cold." Gerard explained as he poured.

"I was just about to ask where she was."

"She's upstairs in bed."

"We've been taking her soup and orange juice," Cameron chimed in as he brought Teresa one of his games. "Do you want to play?"

"Not right now," she said, smiling warmly. "I can't stay very long. I just wanted to talk to you about something." She looked at Gerard and her brown eyes added "alone."

"Cameron, why don't you go up and check on Ava. She might like for you to read to her." Gerard patted his head. "I'll come up and get you."

"Okay. See you later, Ms. Teresa."

Gerard waited until he heard Ava's door close before he sat down beside Teresa. "What's going on?"

"On my way over here I thought I had some good news for you. Now I'm not so sure," said Teresa. She looked down at the floor and sat her coffee cup on the table.

"What?"

"I got a call yesterday from Luis and Alma Fuentes. Luis is Leon's cousin. They've expressed an interest in having Cameron come and live with them."

"But—" Gerard shut his eyes for a minute to stop the room from spinning. "No, I want him to live here. That's what he wants, and it's what his mother wants too," Gerard said, remembering to breathe.

"In most cases where there is a temporary guardian appointed by the court, we continue looking for permanent placement for the child."

"You've already found it here."

"Dr. Wright, they are his relatives. With his mother being sentenced to 10 years, wouldn't it be better—?"

"No, it wouldn't. I want him to stay here, permanently. It doesn't matter to me how long the sentence is. I'm prepared for Cameron to grow up here."

"I can see you've grown quite attached to him and I appreciate your feelings but—"

"I won't," Gerard said, as he took a deep breath. "What are my options if I don't want to give him up?"

"You'd have to go to court. But judges usually place children in this kind of situation with relatives." Teresa looked into his eyes for a moment. "Off the record, Dr. Wright, I wouldn't go that route. If it were me, I would try to arrange a meeting with the relatives and talk them out of pursuing custody. In court you'll lose." She took a card out of her purse. "Here's their contact information. Don't—"

"I won't mention what you said, but thank you so much for the advice."

"You're welcome," she said and sighed. "I have to get going."

"Thank you again," Gerard said at the front door.

"Good luck to you. I can see how happy Cameron is here and I'd really like to see him stay that way."

"I'm not going to give him up, ever," Gerard said just before he watched her drive away. He saw that Ava's door was still closed upstairs and sat down at his desk. The phone rang three times before David answered.

"Hello."

"Hello David, it's Gerard. I'm sorry to call so early."

"It's not too early. We were at a fundraiser pretty late last night. Besides, when my private line rings, I know something is wrong. What's happened?"

"It's Cameron. Some of his relatives have come forward and they want to take him away."

"Gerard, I can tell by your voice that you're very upset right now. But if you think about it, isn't this a good thing?" David asked, his voice calm.

"No, no I don't!" Gerard didn't realize how upset he was. "I'm sorry."

"Just try to calm down."

"I want you to set up a meeting with them so I can tell them I want to keep Cameron. I have the phone number."

"Gerard…"

"David please, we have to act quickly."

"All right, give me the information. I'll see what I can do." David said in an even tone although his mind was already racing onto his next phone call.

"We have a problem," he said as soon as there was an answer.

"What is going on?" The soft melodious voice asked.

"He wants to meet with you. He wants to keep the kid."

"But you said..."

"Alma, I know what I said," David interrupted. "Don't get distracted by all this. We already have a deal. Meet with him and tell him you want the boy. Tell him you'll go to court if you have to. I'll take it from there."

"Okay. I'll tell Luis," said Alma, as she watched her husband come in from the porch where he had been smoking.

"Tell Luis what?" he asked after she hung up the phone. He ran his fingers through his short, dark brown hair and sat down beside her, blinking his blue eyes.

"That was David on the phone," she said, tracing his square jaw with her finger. "It seems that the guy wants to keep Cameron more than he thought he would."

"How much does he want him?"

"He wants to see us and beg." Alma laughed.

"But Alma." Luis stopped laughing. "Don't you see what this means?"

She shook her head.

"If this guy wants to keep Cameron, he'll pay a pretty penny. We could name our price."

"But Luis..." Alma began just before he pulled her closer and kissed her soft red lips. In that moment she remembered why they had gotten involved with David Boudreau's scheme in the first place. All they had to do was get custody of Cameron and David would give them $10,000 more than he already had.

"Why not? We could collect our money and leave. We could go down to Florida like you wanted, and start over." Luis closed his blue eyes for a moment. "I bet you would even feel like singing again in Miami."

"It's not that I don't feel like it," Alma said, looking away. "I can't."

"Of course you can. Your voice is still there. Look Alma, we need a break. If you've got a better idea, let's hear it."

"I don't like double crossing him. How do you think he's going to take that?"

"There's nothing he can do about it. Besides, we'll leave the same day we get the 50 grand."

"You think we could get $50,000 out of him?" Alma asked.

"I thought you would see things my way."

"Gerry, I read to Ava for awhile. She's going to sleep again." Cameron came to Gerard's desk with a book. "Do you want to hear the story now?"

"I'd love to. Go ahead." He began to fill his pipe with tobacco. He smiled as Cameron climbed into the massive leather chair across from his. He looked like they were about to have a serious business meeting. Gerard liked to hear Cameron read. The tutor, Lisa Johnson, had uncovered another of Cameron's talents. He could read on a sixth-grade level even though he was only seven years old. She was so excited that she gave him an IQ test the first week of his lessons. Gerard already knew that Cameron was a genius, now she did also.

"Can I strike the match?" Cameron was watching him with great interest.

"Certainly not, and I don't want you to ever play with matches." Gerard lit the pipe with one of the long wooden matches from his desk drawer. A few moments later, the sweet aromatic tobacco began to faintly scent the room. He usually only smoked at night after Cameron had gone to bed, but today he needed to calm down early.

"Is something wrong Gerry?" Cameron put the book down.

"There's nothing for you to worry about," Gerard said and blew a smoke ring. He realized how worried his face must look.

"Do it again!" Cameron said, as he watched the ring fade out of sight over his head. Gerard blew another just as the phone rang.

"Hello, David?"

"No Gerard, it's Alan."

"Sorry. I was expecting a call." He glanced over to find Cameron watching him. "Why don't you go watch TV for a few minutes?"

"Okay." Cameron looked disappointed as he left the room.

"Are you there Gerard?" Alan asked.

"Yes, sorry about that. I've been trying to get in touch with you."

"I've been over in Biloxi," said Alan. He sounded like he was still half asleep. "I need to talk to you. Could I come over?"

"No." Gerard said abruptly. He thought about how Cameron had reacted to Alan in the mall. "I'm busy today. Tomorrow, come to my office. I've wanted to talk to you, too."

Alan sighed. "I've got some session work in the morning, but I could come in the afternoon."

"Tomorrow afternoon then," Gerard said and hung up the phone. What could Alan want to talk to him about? He certainly had some questions for him.

Gerard found Cameron frowning at the TV screen. "I thought we were going to watch cartoons," he said, patting him on the head.

"Something else is on, the weatherman."

"What is it?" Gerard sat down beside him.

"A tornado warning is in effect for the entire viewing area. Stay tuned throughout the day because there is even more severe weather headed our way tonight."

"Gerry?"

"Oh, we'll be fine here. This house is more than 100 years old," Gerard said. "We even have an emergency plan."

"We do?"

"This bathroom downstairs is extra secure and we would get in the bathtub and cover up with a mattress. If a tornado came our way, we would be just fine," Gerard said.

Cameron did not look convinced.

Gerard spent the rest of the day with Cameron. He played three different video games and watched several cartoon videos to try and take Cameron's mind off of the weather. The only thing that seemed to work, however, was when he asked Cameron to make up a "concert" for him. This game brightened his tense mood right away because music spoke to him in a way that nothing else could. Gerard loved listening to him play a list of his favorites. He applauded after every number and Cameron took a bow. Several hours passed quickly as they amused themselves this way. Late in the afternoon, Ava came downstairs in the dark blue Turkish bathrobe he had given her for Christmas.

"I'm sorry that you've had to do my work for me these past few days," Ava said to Gerard as she walked into the music room where Cameron was playing Beethoven.

"Come sit down. You shouldn't be down here. I'm glad you're feeling a little better, but you don't want to overdo it," Gerard said quietly and patted a pillow for her on the sofa.

"Who can stay in bed with this beautiful music filling the house?" She looked at Cameron and smiled.

"Hi Ava, are you better now?" Cameron asked a few minutes later after he had finished the sonata. He climbed down from the piano bench and went to sit between Ava and Gerard.

"Just a little." She put her arms around him. "I'm sorry I haven't been able to do things with you this week. But I promise you that next week we'll have a lot of fun together."

"You can help me with my new building set," Cameron said. He smiled broadly when she hugged him.

"Why don't we order in tonight?" Gerard asked before he went into the kitchen. He returned a moment later with a handful of menus. "Everyone take their pick, whatever you want." He placed the menus on the coffee table and watched delight spread across Cameron's face. "If I didn't know better, I'd think you were getting tired of my cooking."

Cameron looked down at the floor and blushed, but he shook his head "no." Gerard began to laugh as he realized that he needed to learn a few recipes that were more appropriate to the tastes of a 7 year old.

The dining service brought them nachos, hamburgers, and

Chinese food. They each enjoyed their separate meals.

Cameron began to look tired around 8 o'clock and he did not make it to the end of his favorite "Indiana Jones" action movie. Ava followed Gerard as he carried Cameron upstairs and put him to bed.

They had all gone to bed by 11, but the storm was just getting started. Gerard lay in the darkness listening to the wind howling. The torrential rain came down in sheets against the roof. Then he heard something new: it sounded like buckets of rocks were being dropped on the roof, and the volume was overpowering. It was so loud that he did not hear the sound of the kitchen door being forced open.

Cameron tossed in his bed, unable to wake himself from his nightmare.

> *He was coming again. Cameron knew the sound of his footsteps. He could hear him on the steps outside. Cameron sat up on the couch where he had been sleeping and opened his mouth to scream mama!, but no sound would come out. He was too scared.*
>
> *The footsteps were getting closer. Cameron sprang off the couch and ran into his mother's room. "Where did she go?" Cameron could not believe that she was not there and Daddy was coming back again. Hot tears rolled down his face as he crawled into his hiding place.*
>
> *"Magdalene!" Leon de la Valle yelled as he dropped down on the sofa. The house was warm so he took off his black leather jacket. He ran his slender fingers through his long, dark brown hair. "Where the hell are you?" he growled and waited a moment. "My head hurts," he whispered and leaned his head back until it touched the cement wall. He closed his emerald green eyes.*

Cameron was so frightened that he could hardly breathe. He could see his father, there on the couch, and prayed that he would go to sleep until his mother got home. It was dark and cold under the bed, but he would wait there until she came back.

A smile formed on Leon's lips. He put his hands over his eyes in peek-a-boo fashion and said, "I see you." He laughed.

Cameron stopped breathing when he realized his father was looking right at him. He was paralyzed as he watched the black shoes come towards the bed, then stop. He waited. All at once, he was face to face with his father. Leon lay down on the floor beside the bed and smiled. Cameron could hear himself crying when he looked at that sinister grin.

"Now is that any way to greet me?" he asked gently, but his grasp was excruciating when he grabbed Cameron's arm and began to pull him from under the bed. He kicked and struggled, but it was useless. It was like trying to fight a giant. Seconds later, his father was standing up with him, holding him in a vise-like embrace. "Shut up!"

"Please, Daddy," he said, sobbing.

"I said, shut up." Leon's voice was barely above a whisper. He took a deep breath and put him down. Cameron stood trembling. "Don't be scared. I just want to talk to you." He sat on the bed. "Where's Mama?"

"I don't know," said Cameron. His voice shook as he slowly backed away. His father's glowing eyes seem to look right through him and he stared at him for a moment that seemed like an eternity.

"Bring me the aspirin bottle and a cup of water," said Leon as he reclined across the bed.

Cameron's fears began to subside as he went to the

kitchen drawer and got out the clear bottle that read "aspirin."

It would be all right this time, he thought. He would just be quiet and let his father sleep until his mother returned. He would be okay. It wouldn't be like the other times that she was not home. Cameron took the bottle and a white coffee mug filled with tap water, back to the bedroom. Leon was lying so still that Cameron thought he was already sleeping. He looked over at the night stand for a place to set the cup when Leon suddenly sprang up from the bed. He grabbed him with both hands. The cup smashed into pieces on the cement floor, along with the aspirin bottle. Cameron tried to pull away. "No!" he screamed.

"What's the matter? You act like you don't love me anymore." Leon put his hand over his son's mouth and sat him on his lap.

Cameron continued to try to scream underneath the hand, until the room faded into darkness.

"No! Don't!" Cameron awoke and sat up in his bed. There was a ferocious roar all around him and then his light went out. He began to scream.

"Cameron! Cameron, I'm coming!" Gerard's blood went cold when he heard the child screaming. He reached for the flashlight that he kept in his night stand and ran to Cameron's room. He shined the beam of light at the bed where Cameron sat with the comforter pulled around him, screaming. Gerard put the light down on the floor and tried to put his arms around him.

"No!" he screamed again and swung wildly, catching Gerard just below his left eye.

"Ouch!" Gerard put his hand over his eye instinctively. He shook off the pain and took a deep breath. "Cameron, it's me, Gerry. I'm not going to hurt you." He spoke loudly so he could be heard over the noise outside. He picked up the flashlight and pointed it at the ceiling between them. Cameron looked up at the light, his chest heaving.

"What is that?"

"It's hail, little balls of ice. It'll be over soon," Gerard said. He wanted him to calm down so he would stop hyperventilating.

"It's dark,." Cameron said and sobbed. "He's—"

"The power went out. It's a bad storm. Are you all right?"

Cameron nodded.

"Let's go sit with Ava. She has a battery powered radio."

"Okay," Cameron said and reached out to him.

Gerard was relieved that the boy allowed him to pick him up. Cameron held the flashlight as they went down the hall to Ava's room. She was not in her bed or her bathroom.

"Ava!" Gerard called down the dark hall in the direction of his room. He was just about to call again when the hail stopped and a shrill siren replaced it. Cameron jumped.

"Gerry!"

"It's the tornado siren. We have to get downstairs." Gerard ran carefully in the beam of the flashlight down the stairs. "Ava! Ava!" he yelled all the way to the bathroom. He placed Cameron in the tub and headed for the door.

"No! Don't leave me!" Cameron screamed.

Gerard stood in the doorway, torn between looking for Ava and staying with Cameron. "Ava! Ava!" He called to her, but she did not come. "Ava, please take cover." He thought. He jumped into the tub just as he heard a ferocious wind blowing. He covered Cameron and waited while he heard the wind tearing at the house. It sounded like a train was coming straight for them. A few minutes later, all was quiet. "Cameron, are you okay?"

"Yes."

"Come on," Gerard said as he pulled Cameron out of the tub and carried him down the hall. There was no interior damage. He would check the outside in the morning. "Let's find Ava," Gerard said. He carried the child into the kitchen. There was nowhere else to look.

"There she is," said Cameron, pointing towards the floor by the table.

Gerard put him down. "Wait right here."

"No."

"You hold the flashlight, but stand right here." Gerard said. His heart pounded harder and harder in his chest. He walked over and kneeled beside her. He thought that she must have fainted. Then he checked for her pulse. There was none. It was only then that he noticed the tiny pool of blood collected underneath
her. "Oh my God!" he exclaimed before he put his hand over his mouth.

"Gerry, what is it?"

"Just stay there," Gerard said as he reached for the phone on the wall. There was no dial tone.

PART II

Chapter Eight

"Gerry, what's happening?" Cameron sobbed. The beam from the flashlight drooped to the floor and shone on Ava's bare feet.

"Just stay where you are." Gerard tried to sound calm. He hung up the phone and started towards Cameron when he saw something out of the corner of his eye. There in the darkness, he could see someone standing in the hallway, behind Cameron. Gerard could hardly breathe as he inched closer to the child. Would the killer go after him next?

"Gerry," Cameron began, but he did not get out another word before Gerard grabbed him and raced to the garage door. "What are you doing?"

"Shhh," Gerard said as he shut the door behind them. He pushed the button for the garage door opener. He had forgotten how much noise it made as it slowly opened. Whoever was inside would certainly know where they were. "Get in." Once they were inside the Mercedes, he shuffled through the glove compartment and took out the leather zippered case that contained his 9mm handgun. He heard Cameron gasp when he took out the gun. "I think there's someone in the house," he whispered. "You wait here."

"No," Cameron begged in a strained whisper and grabbed his pajama sleeve. "Don't go."

Gerard breathed a long sigh as he picked up the car phone and dialed 911. If he was not able to subdue whoever was inside the house, Cameron would be left alone with the killer. He could never let that happen.

"911 emergency."

"Someone has broken into my house. They're still here. I think they have already killed my housekeeper." Gerard said quietly as he glanced at Cameron, who looked back at him with frightened eyes.

"We've traced your address, sir. The police are on their way. They'll be there in the next three or four minutes. Can you get out of the house or are you in a safe place to hide?"

"We're in the car in the garage." Gerard said and started the engine of the Mercedes. "I can drive down the street."

"That's a good idea. Just try to remain calm. Why don't you stay on the line until the police get there?"

"Okay. I'm going to drive down the street now. Maybe I'll meet the police at the corner and—" Gerard was saying when a high-pitched scream broke through the quiet car. "Cameron, what is it?"

"Back there! Gerry, it's Daddy!" Cameron cried.

Gerard saw a tall thin figure run deftly across the yard in the rain just as flashing blue lights came into sight from the other direction. The sudden hail had ended but the little pieces of ice formed a thin layer over the ground.

"Sir! What's going on?" The voice on the phone line yelled.

"The police are here now. Thank you." Gerard said and hung up the car phone. "Cameron, calm down. It's not him," he said as he backed the car into the driveway and stopped. The police pulled in behind him. Cameron was beginning to hyperventilate just as the lanky patrolman carefully walked to the car to avoid slipping on the ice.

"Mr. Wright? Are you the one who called the police about a break-in?"

"Yes," said Gerard as he opened the car door and pulled Cameron out with him. "Cameron, calm down. Breathe slowly."

"Wait here sir," said the officer, whose badge read "R. Grange." "Did you get in a fight with the man?" He asked as he looked at Gerard's face. He motioned towards his eye.

Gerard looked at his reflection in the car window and saw the bruise on his face. Cameron had given him a black eye. He shook his head. "No, I just saw him run across the yard that way. He was wearing some kind of mask."

"Who hit you?" Officer Grange asked.

"He was having a nightmare when I woke him." Gerard looked down at Cameron who was breathing calmly.

"Do you know how many there were?"

"I don't know. I only saw the one."

"Okay. Taylor, that way," he called to his partner and he ran down the street in the direction Gerard had given. "You stay out here. I'm going inside to look around." He drew his gun just as a few lights came on in the house.

"The backup generator finally came on."

Cameron looked up at Gerard. His emerald green eyes looked terrified. "What's happening Gerry? Is Ava going to be all right?"

"I'm sorry, precious, but I don't think she will be," Gerard said. He picked Cameron up and hugged him. "She's gone."

"It was Daddy," he whispered.

"Cameron, your father is dead. It wasn't him." He pulled him away for a moment to look into his face. "I don't know who that was, but it wasn't your father. You believe me don't you?"

Cameron did not answer.

"I saw someone running, but I lost him two blocks over," Officer Taylor said, breathing heavily as he walked up the driveway towards them. Another police car pulled up to the curb and the two policemen went into the house.

Over two hours later Gerard sat in the living room with Cameron and talked to Detective Fisher. The kitchen had been dusted for fingerprints; Ava's body had been photographed and taken away in the coroner's van. Gerard had wanted to stay in the kitchen, but it was not the place for Cameron.

"I need to ask you a few questions for my report," said Detective Fisher. He had bright red hair; even his eyebrows and lashes were the same flaming red. "Have you noticed anything missing, Dr.

Wright?" Detective Fisher wrote everything Gerard said down in his little tablet.

"No, not that I can tell. My office has been disturbed, but there's nothing of value in there."

"What did you keep in your office, any prescription pads?" another detective asked from across the room.

"He's not that kind of doctor," Fisher answered and narrowed his blue eyes. "What was in the office?"

"Files about the symphony budget, music, personal notes about musicians and rehearsals. I have a safe upstairs where I keep important things and valuables."

"Do you know who would want to hurt your housekeeper?" He glanced down at Cameron.

"No, I don't. She was his nanny actually," Gerard said and put his arm around Cameron. "She's been with us, or had been, for a couple of months."

"Oh, I see," said Fisher. He smiled at Cameron. "I saw you on TV playing the piano. You're very good."

Cameron smiled shyly and nudged closer to Gerard. "Thank you."

"We need her identification so we can inform her family."

"I'll get her purse upstairs." Gerard stood up. "You know she never mentioned her family. She came here from Atlanta, to go to school."

He was not surprised when Cameron followed him up the stairs. Cameron had been hyperventilating earlier and now he only wanted to keep him calm. They had both cried when the paramedics covered Ava's body and took her out of the kitchen. Unfortunately, Gerard did not have to explain about death to Cameron. He already knew.

Ava's small leather purse was sitting on her dresser. Gerard picked Cameron up for the trip back downstairs. He was exhausted himself; he could only imagine how tired a 7-year-old boy must feel.

Detective Fisher opened the purse on the coffee table in the living room. Gerard lay Cameron down on the sofa and sat beside him. The usual contents were placed on the table: lipstick, powder, a comb, and keys. Then Fisher took out a wallet.

"Her Georgia driver's license says she's 24. Does that sound right to you?"

"Yes." Gerard glanced at the small photo on the ID. "Ava Carter? She said her name was Anderson."

"Anderson." Fisher frowned at his notebook. "We'll have to check this out, of course. There may be some simple explanation." He put the top on his pen. "We understand it's very late. All our preliminary work is finished. The team is finished in the kitchen. We will need you to come down to headquarters and make an official statement in the morning. But for tonight, we are going to let you get some rest."

Gerard walked him to the door and left Cameron sleeping. "This is terrible. I don't know what we'll do without her. She was like a part of the family," Gerard said as his throat tightened.

"We're going to find whoever did this, Dr. Wright," Fisher said and shook his hand. "There will be a patrol car out front all night, so you rest easy. We'll see you in the morning. Goodnight."

"Goodnight," Gerard said and waited near the door as all the police filed out of his house. He had seen more police in the past three months than he had in the past three years. But he knew that was not what was bothering him the most, as he locked up and carried Cameron upstairs. He decided to let Cameron sleep in his room. After a night like this, he shouldn't have to wake up alone. He gently put him down and went to the night stand on the other side of the bed. He sat down and slid the drawer open quietly.

The brown leather photo album was beginning to show wear for the 11 years he had kept it. Inside were the photos that he always kept near him, but out of sight. His wife and Ava could have been twins, they looked so much alike. Tears rolled down his face as he turned the pages slowly.

He took the album with him downstairs to the bar where he poured himself a whiskey. He sank down in his oversized leather chair and sat the bottle beside him on the coffee table, just in case he wanted another. He could allow himself a drink, after a night like this, he thought. Gerard remembered the last time he'd found a woman dead. It was his wife Elizabeth.

Gerard had known Elizabeth since they were 15. They had both been entered in the same piano competition in London. He lost the prize, but won her heart. They kept in touch with letters and phone calls, but this first love was none the less real for both of them.

The romance almost came to an abrupt halt when they were 17 and she was invited to study at Juilliard. Gerard had not been invited, but he could go to an open audition, if she wanted him to. Elizabeth told Gerard that although it wasn't so bad having a relationship across the distance to Dublin, where she lived, it just wouldn't be possible for them to go on if she was in New York and he was in London.

Gerard had survived her mood swings over the two years they dated, but today she was more morose than ever. And that was when he'd said it. "I could go with you. We could be married." It was as simple as that. They did not give it much thought, but then with first love, you didn't have to.

Their parents were a different matter. Elizabeth's were in shock. They seemed to adopt the attitude that if they ignored the situation, it would go away. They could not believe that their daughter would get married without their permission. Gerard's father was a lot more direct and vocal. He warned him that if he went to America with a new bride, he would do it without any money from him. The words "I'll cut you off without a penny!" were supposed to be enough to scare him into not going through with it.

But the words were not enough. Gerard and Elizabeth were married at the office of the justice of the peace the same day their plane left for New York. Gerard had aced the open audition in London and if he performed as well in New York, he would be offered a spot at the prestigious school of music. Gerard's talents lay in composing music, and he hoped that New York would give him an audience for his work.

Elizabeth was his biggest supporter, always listening and critiquing his latest creations.

Gerard poured himself another drink and almost smiled when he thought about her thick blonde hair cut in a bob and those warm brown eyes, but then he remembered how she died.

Juilliard had been a complete disaster for both of them. Elizabeth could not handle the pressure of the school, and every week she became more depressed and laconic. The only thing she had energy to do was smother Gerard. The more she clung to him, the more he wanted to get away. In their long distance relationship, there was still so much that he hadn't known about her. He did not even know what manic depression was, but he did after a month in New York.

She was a better pianist than he when she felt like playing, which was not very often. Gerard's father hadn't given him any money, but his mother consented to a gift, against his father's wishes, to go along with his continued allowance. Gerard was heir to her estate after all—his father was not. Sometimes, in the Wright household it was easy to forget who held the purse strings because his mother was kind and generous and continued to let her husband run things even after he had lost his personal fortune in one bad business deal after another.

His mother was told she had cancer two months after Gerard moved to New York. While she was in the hospital, she granted his father, Thomas, power of attorney. The first thing Thomas did was cut off Gerard's funds. No 17-year-old son of his was going to disobey him, marry some high-strung girl who he could not support, and expect him to give them money. Thomas had told Gerard dozens of times that he was never going to amount to anything in music. Gerard had always thought that any time Thomas got the opportunity to cut him down, he seized it.

Gerard started playing in clubs that he was too young to even be in. Within weeks, he had begun his on again-off again love affair with alcohol.

A wave of guilt went through him and he put his glass down. It didn't slow his thoughts, though.

"Where have you been?" Elizabeth was sitting on the red velvet sofa in her white terry bathrobe. "I was up all night." She lunged at him when he got closer to her. "Worrying about you!" she screamed and they both crashed down on the hard wood floor when Gerard lost his balance. "I hate you! I hate you!" Her fists pounded his chest.

"Stop!" Gerard tried to grab her hands. "Stop it!" He rolled her over and grabbed one of her hands just before she landed a punch with the other. "What the hell is wrong with you?" He held both her hands this time.

She panted for breath then her eyes filled with tears. "Let me go," she moaned.

"You haven't been taking your medication have you?" Gerard moved away from her and sat on the floor in front of the sofa.

"I've been working, you know that." Then the silence lay there between them for a long time.

"You should have told me."

"Told you what?" Elizabeth rolled over and looked at him. "How did you find out?"

Gerard suddenly felt more exhausted than he had in all his 18 years. "I meant you should have told me you were manic depressive before we got married." He leaned his head back against the seat cushions and looked up at the ceiling. The heat was on, but he was shivering. "And now I'm broke, because of you. My mother is in the hospital and I can't see her, because of you." He was surprised to feel a hot tear roll down his cheek. "You've turned down two paid recitals this month already, because you didn't feel like it." He wiped the tears away. "You act like an hysterical child, and all we ever do is argue. And you say you hate me."

"Gerard…"

"I wish I had never come here." He stood up. "I'm going to start with my aunt and work my way down a list until I find someone who will loan me enough money to get back to England!"

"You're not leaving me here!" Elizabeth sat up. As usual, her mood changed instantly. Now instead of being sorrowful, she was angry.

"You just watch me!" He raced to the door and she was right behind him.

"You can't. We're going to have a baby!"

"A what? Are you crazy?" Gerard seethed. "I guess you don't need to answer that."

"Where are you going?" She grabbed his arm.

"I already told you! This is your problem. I can't deal with this right now!" Gerard jerked his arm from her grasp and ran back out into the night he had just come in from.

The half melted snow had turned into a gray dirty sludge on the New York sidewalks. Gerard pulled on the hood of his black parka as he walked. He bought a calling card at the 24-hour drugstore and went to the phone in the back of the store. He found his family attorney's home number in his tiny address book.

"Hello, Mr. Carton?" he asked unsure.

"Gerard Wright, where on earth are you calling from? I couldn't believe it when my maid said it was you."

"I'm in New York." Gerard couldn't afford to waste the minutes on his calling card. "Mr. Carton, I want to get a loan against my trust fund."

"You can't until you turn 18."

"That's not until March."

"That's the way it's arranged. Perhaps you should come in and we can talk about it."

"But that's the problem." Gerard tried to stay calm. "I want to come home." His voice broke as he finished. "I don't have access to any money—"

"Gerard are you in trouble?"

"It's just that my mother is in the hospital and I'm so far away. Father cut off my allowance."

"May I ask why?"

"Well, he didn't want me to get married." Gerard answered and realized what he had just said. What was he doing here in this drugstore?

"Married, who did you marry? When?" Carton began excitedly.

"I'm going to have to call you back. I've got to go home." Gerard began to smile to himself. "I've got an apology to make." He thought of Elizabeth's beautiful brown eyes. "Thanks for listening."

"Gerard, this is all quite odd, but call me back whenever you need to. I'll help you any way that I can."

"Thank you." Gerard hung up the phone and rushed out of the store so quickly that the clerk frowned, sure that he must have stolen something. He ran most of the five blocks back to his apartment building. The elevator seemed to take an eternity to climb to the tenth floor.

"Elizabeth," he called as soon as he was inside, but there was no answer. "Oh there you are." He saw her lying across the bed, face down. "Hey there, wake up long enough to let me apologize." He shook her, and then turned her over when she didn't respond. It was then that he saw the broken mirror glass in her hand. As his eyes traveled over her, he saw the blood-soaked robe and her gray skin. Blood wasn't still pouring out of her neck where she had cut herself, but leaked slowly, after death. He was too late.

"Elizabeth!" he screamed. "No!" He held her close to him and rock back and forth. "I'm sorry. I'm sorry," he whispered.

Gerard sank down further in his chair, there in the living room, and cried himself to sleep.

Chapter Nine

He ran as fast as he could across the front yard. He had no choice but to keep going, even though they would see him. Of course they would see him run past the garage, but there was no other way back to his car. Everything was supposed to be perfect. He had planned how he would break into the house, get the folder, and leave while they were all still sleeping.

He kept thinking as he was running, though. "Why did she have to come downstairs? Why?" He knew the policeman was behind him, so he ran faster, not even caring if he slipped on the balls of ice. None of it mattered much now anyway. He hadn't gotten what he went there for, and worse he'd had to kill the girl. He winced at the thought of the bloody knife in his pocket. He never wanted to hurt anybody. He could tell from the look on her face that she was just about to start screaming, and he couldn't let her do that.

When he turned the corner onto Prytania, he noticed that the policeman had given up, so he slowed down a little. His car was waiting for him just as he'd left it. By the time he got in, the hail had already started to melt. A murderer. He said aloud, "I'm a murderer now." This was not what he had planned. He had never killed anyone before, not even Leon, although he had tried. He waited for the ice to melt a little more before he started the car. The last thing he would need was a traffic accident now.

With his eyes squeezed tight to block out the memory of what had just happened, he thought about the music. Leon de la Valle had written so many songs while they were together that he had taken it for granted that he would not mind selling him some of them. That was why he had already started passing the compositions off as his own to that record producer. Of course, Leon had always been unpredictable, but he couldn't believe how violently he had reacted when he found out. He had actually been afraid that Leon was going to kill him. But it didn't turn out that way.

He began the drive back to his place. When he reached the lakefront, he hurled the knife into the water. He couldn't stop now, though. He had killed for it. He knew that he would have to find another way back in to get that music, before the kid remembered anything about that night.

Something soft touching his cheek woke Gerard the next morning. He slowly opened his eyes and saw the sun streaming through the living room window. The pain in his head was excruciating, and he still felt something annoying him. It was the feel a series of gentle taps from a child's hand on his cheek. He squinted at Cameron.

"Gerry, Gerry wake up." Cameron stopped when he saw Gerard's eyes blink open. "Someone's at the door. Do you want me to get it?"

"What? What?" Gerard asked groggily and squeezed his eyes shut again. Then the doorbell rang again.

"Do you want me to see who it is?"

"No." Gerard sat up and knocked over the empty whiskey bottle. The room swayed. "I'll get it." He steadied himself as he walked to the front door. When he looked through the peephole he saw a woman and man walking away.

"Yes." He said after he opened the door and they turned to face him. A feeling of fear crept into him. The man's coloring reminded him of Leon de la Valle.

"Dr. Wright?" The woman's voice was soft and musical. She continued when Gerard nodded. "I'm Alma Fuentes, this is my husband Luis. We're—"

"I know who you are, but what are you doing here? Did my lawyer call you?" Gerard tried to get a good look at the couple. The woman, Alma, looked to be in her late twenties, with shoulder-length black hair and brown eyes. She had beautiful, bee stung lips that Gerard couldn't help but notice.

"Yes, he did. He didn't tell you we were coming?"

Gerard ran his hand through his black hair and took a deep breath. This was just perfect he thought. "They want to take him away from me and I'm standing here with a hangover."

He stepped aside. "Won't you come in?" he asked.

"Thank you." Alma said and Luis walked in behind her. He gave Gerard's hand a firm shake.

"The living room is right through there." Gerard motioned towards the doorway on the right. "Go ahead and make yourselves comfortable. I'll be with you in just a minute." He watched them go inside and then went to the den doorway where Cameron had been standing, watching.

Gerard suddenly felt very nervous about the people in the living room. He didn't even want Cameron to know who they were. "We have some company. Why don't you come upstairs with me?"

"Okay. Is something wrong, Gerry?"

"No. Nothing." Gerard tried to sound calm. He carried Cameron upstairs to save time. "You can watch television for a little while. When they leave, I'll make you some breakfast," he called from the bathroom while he splashed cold water on his face, carefully avoiding his black eye, and brushed his teeth. He splashed and then combed his wavy black hair and within ten minutes headed downstairs looking and feeling a little better.

He went into the kitchen and started the coffee maker. "I'm sorry about that. We had some trouble here last night. I hardly slept." Gerard said as he went into the living room.

"We went to your office at 8:30 like the lawyer said." Luis said as he looked around the room. "Cameron is looking well." He stared directly at Gerard.

"What happened last night?" Alma asked before he could respond.

"We had a break-in. My housekeeper was killed."

"Housekeeper is a very dangerous job at this house. They have some really rotten luck." Luis laughed until Alma narrowed her eyes at him. "Sorry."

"Cameron wasn't—"

"No, Cameron was never in any danger." Gerard winced as his mind flashed back to how close the killer had been standing to the child.

"Is that what happened to your face?" Luis asked.

Gerard hesitated. "Well, no, in the confusion Cameron woke up swinging." Gerard smiled. "Do you want some coffee?"

"That would be nice," Alma said warmly.

Gerard rolled the silver coffee service set in as quickly as he could. As they poured their coffee, Alma looked around the room. "You do have a beautiful home, Dr. Wright. But we came to talk about Cameron. Luis and I realize that Magdalene won't be out of prison for a long time. It seems the right thing to do for Cameron is to let him stay with us since he doesn't have much family."

"I know that you're his relatives, but Magdalene asked me to take care of him, and that's what I want to do." Gerard paused to breathe. "Cameron is very happy here."

"But we're—"Alma began.

"Fifty grand." Luis interrupted.

"What?" Gerard sat his cup down.

"If you want to keep him, it will cost you $50,000," Luis said, staring at Gerard with sparkling blue eyes.

"Are you serious?"

"There's no point wasting any more time with this. That's what Alma and I want. No court would let you keep him instead of us, anyway. This is a dangerous environment. I can imagine why Magdalene wanted him to stay here, but with everything that goes on," Luis motioned towards the empty whiskey bottle on the floor.

Gerard froze. He couldn't believe that he had forgotten it. He picked it up and took it to the bar. "All right. I'll give it to you. But I want it in writing that you won't ask to have him back again later."

He turned to face them and looked from Luis to Alma. "Will you sign?"

"Of course." Luis answered. Alma did not meet his gaze. "I guess we better be going. Can we finish our transaction this afternoon?"

"This afternoon is fine. Come back to my office around 3. I'll have the check ready."

"We'll see you then."

Gerard walked them to the door in silence. He watched them drive away in a small black car.

"How was that?" Luis asked once they pulled out of the driveway.

"You were great." Alma gave him a half-hearted smile.

"You're not still worried about David are you?"

"No, he can't stop us without exposing himself, whatever he's up to. It's just Cameron, did you see him?"

"Yeah, I saw him when we first came in. He was in a doorway down the hall."

"He looked so sweet. He has Leon's eyes."

"I know he's a cute kid and everything Alma, but we have other plans. Remember Miami?" Luis glanced over at her as he turned onto St. Charles.

"I know, but…"

"Did you see that house? It's a mansion. Gerard Wright is rich and he's obviously crazy about the kid. Why take him away from that?"

"Someone was murdered there last night."

"It must have been a robbery. So they'll get a new alarm system and everyone will be safe. Stop worrying." Luis waited for Alma to respond. "What's wrong?"

"Don't you even want to see him again?"

"No, I don't. If we take this money, Alma, we won't be seeing him again."

"He didn't say we couldn't see him just that we can't try to get custody."

"Alma, I don't think it's a good idea," Luis said, and they rode on in silence. "All right. We can ask about it, but if he says no, let's just drop it."

"Okay." Alma said and a slight smile formed on her lips.

"What did cousin Alma want?" Cameron asked when Gerard opened his bedroom door. Instead of watching cartoons, he was reading a chapter book.

"You saw them come in?" Gerard sat down beside him when Cameron looked at him and nodded. "Were you close to cousin Alma?"

"Sometimes she was my babysitter when Mama had to work. It was before she came to work here."

"Oh, I see." Gerard suddenly felt worried. "You like it here, Cameron?"

Cameron nodded. "I love you Gerry."

"I love you too." Gerard's eyes grew red. "Are you ready for breakfast?" he asked, changing the subject.

"Yeah."

"Come on downstairs then and we'll find something." Gerard led the way. "Cameron we have to talk about something."

"Ava?"

"How did you know? I'm sorry about what happened to her. It must be pretty scary for you, too. We'll talk about it with your doctor today. I was thinking that we could move to a different house if you're afraid here. Are you?" Gerard asked, as he took out eggs and a skillet.

"I'm not afraid, if you'll be here too." A question flickered in Cameron's eyes. "Do you think Mama will be back soon?"

"I don't know when exactly, but she'll be back. She may not be able to call every day, but we can write her letters. I don't know why I didn't think of it sooner. Do you want to write her today?"

"I'll get started now." Cameron took paper and pens out of the white desk in the kitchen. Then he stared down at the floor where Ava was found the previous night. There were no chalk outlines or tape, but Gerard knew what he was thinking.

"Why don't we go out for breakfast? I have some meetings today after your doctor's appointment, but you can come to the theater with me. I'll make you a snack now, so you can have your insulin." He took out the bread. Maybe tonight we can stay at a hotel." He watched Cameron start to smile.

"I never stayed at a hotel before. Mama worked at one, but we never stayed there."

"Then tonight will be a treat." He spread peanut butter on the toast to make Cameron's favorite snack. Much to Gerard's pleasure, Cameron had stopped his hysterics during insulin injections and the whole process had become quite simple. Cameron sat down to eat his toast.

"Gerry, can we get room service?"

"Don't talk with your mouth full. Yes, we'll even get room service. Now, you go get packed. I'll be up to help you in a minute."

"Okay," he said and disappeared up the stairs.

When Cameron was out of sight, Gerard picked up the phone. An answering machine picked up after he listened to several rings. Gerard hung up and dialed again. This time there was an answer on the second ring.

"Hello."

"Hello, David. It's Gerard. I need to talk to you."

"I'm due in court in an hour. What's wrong?"

"We had a break-in last night. Ava was killed."

"What?" David raised his voice.

"I'm sorry. I know you can't talk right now. But I need you to do something for me before 3 today."

"What is it?"

"I need a document for Cameron's relatives to sign saying that they won't try to get custody later. We made an agreement."

"What kind of an agreement?" David asked slowly.

"I'm going to give them $50,000 and they're going to get out of the picture." Gerard paused. "It's what I want, David."

"Are you crazy? Why would you do that?" David was yelling into the phone.

"David, what's—?"

"What is it with you and that damned kid?" David took a deep breath to calm down. "I'm sorry. I just don't understand this. I hate to see you spend that kind of money on a child who's not even yours. He'd be better off with his own kind, anyway."

"What is the matter with you?" Gerard was shocked. "I don't have to explain anything to you. You can do as I say or I'll find another lawyer."

"I'll come to your office around 2," David said and slammed down the phone. He immediately picked it up again and dialed the number written in his phone book. Luis answered. "I don't know what the hell you think you're doing."

"Well, well David, I thought we might be hearing from you."

"I'm going to—" David seethed.

"You aren't going to do anything,." Luis said. He sat up from the position where he had reclined on the couch. "I wonder how your friend would react if he found out you put Alma and I up to try and get Cameron away from him. I think it might also raise some ethical questions for a lawyer like you, who just happens to be running for office."

"I'll get you back for this. I can be a lot worse than you think." David did not say any more. He knew there was no need. It wouldn't even serve a real purpose to get into a bidding war with Gerard for the Fuentes' loyalty. They obviously would go with the highest bidder, and it was clear that Gerard was prepared to go to any lengths to keep that child.

He had not been lying about being due in court. He cursed when he looked at his watch, quickly gathered his papers and attaché, and headed out of his office.

Gerard's hand was shaking when he hung up the phone. What was wrong with David? He had never known him to act like that. What could he possibly have against him wanting to keep Cameron? He was determined to make him explain himself later. When he went into Cameron's room, he was already putting clothes into his blue backpack. "You're doing a very good job."

"Is it time to go Gerry?"

Gerard looked down into his sparkling green eyes and froze for a moment. He was taking responsibility for another human life, a helpless human, at that. He had not done a very good job of taking care of himself lately. Now he was rushing to take care of this child, no matter what. He felt good about whatever was changing him, but he felt terrible about all the liquor he'd had the night before. He was going to have to do better than that. "In a few minutes, I have to go pack some things for myself." Gerard hurried down the hall to his bedroom.

After breakfast, the first stop was the police station to give his statement. He left Cameron with a female officer while he went over the previous night's events with Detective Fisher. As he spoke, Gerard was thinking that it was a good thing that they saw someone running from the house; otherwise he might be the prime suspect.

"Oh, we've found out a little more about your housekeeper." Fisher said after he collected Gerard's signed account. "She wasn't quite what she appeared."

"What do you mean?"

"We pulled a routine check and her prior arrests came back."

"What arrest?" Gerard stopped putting on his jacket.

"She lived in Atlanta up until a year ago. While she was there she got brought in on solicitation charges. It was a big sting operation."

"I don't understand." Gerard got the feeling that he was not going to like hearing what the detective had to say.

"She was part of a prostitution ring. It was an expensive set-up. It looked classy and the girls were some of the highest paid that the department had ever been able to find out about. Her madam had enough lawyers to get the case plea bargained down. Ava was one of the ones whose charges were dropped."

"I can't believe this." Gerard was stunned into silence for a moment. "Why would she want to be a nanny?"

"It doesn't really sound like her line of work," Fisher said. "Maybe she was trying to change. Or my guess is she was trying to hide from someone, and maybe last night they found her. A girl like that probably had a lot of dirt on a lot of people." He shook his head. "We're working on this. We'll keep you informed."

"Thank you." Gerard shook hands with the detective.

"I'll let them know we're finished in here." Fisher left the door to the claustrophobic interview room ajar when he went out. Gerard heard two sets of footsteps a minute later.

"Gerry." Cameron came over and hugged him.

"Come on let's go. This is no place for you." Gerard knew how uncomfortable this police station must make him.

"Did you get in trouble?" The worry showed on Cameron's face. Gerard turned around to talk to him before he started the car.

"No, I didn't get into trouble. I just had to tell the police what happened last night so they can find out who did it."

"Maybe it was Daddy. Maybe he was looking for me."

"I—" Gerard paused when he realized that this was a delusion that his psychiatrist would be better to deal with. "I won't let anyone hurt you Cameron, I promise." Gerard watched him nod in agreement.

"Good morning Dr. Wright. You asked to see me before I talk with Cameron today?" Dr. Alison Keppler sat a file folder down on her crowded desk. She was petite with red hair and had a calm manner that put one at ease.

"Yes, I know you've only been treating Cameron for a short time."

"Cameron has been through a severe trauma. There's no timetable for when he will get better."

"I didn't really mean it like that." Gerard shifted in his chair, uncomfortable with the fact that the psychiatrist had anticipated his question. "I just want him to be okay. Last night something else happened and I'm afraid he'll be more upset than usual today."

"What?"

"There was a break-in at the house. Ava must have been downstairs and surprised them. She was killed."

"Ava is dead? Oh, this must be terrible for Cameron. Did he see her body? Was he in danger?"

"Whoever killed her was still in the house. He was standing behind Cameron, but he didn't know it. We ran out to the car."

"Does he think it was his father, or the other man?"

"What other man?" Gerard froze.

"It's come out in sessions, I could play some of the tapes if you like, that there was someone else involved."

"Involved how?"

"With the abuse. I've tried to get him to tell me, but he hasn't said who yet. I don't know to what extent this happened, but there is another molester out there who is just as much of a threat to Cameron as his father was." She flipped through the file in front of her. "I asked him to draw in our first sessions because he wouldn't talk to me. Here are the pictures he drew."

Gerard looked at the first one, it was Magdalene and Cameron. The second picture was of Cameron, Magdalene, and a tall dark man that was obviously him. "Oh my God." Gerard gasped when he looked at the third crayon drawing. He frowned as he studied the picture closely. It was a sinister picture containing three figures. One was clearly Cameron himself, the second could have been Leon, but the third figure was a tall man with blonde hair. "I think I know who this is."

Chapter Ten

Gerard was still shaking as he drove with Cameron to the Orpheum Theater after the counseling session. The theater was quiet at noon since there were no rehearsals scheduled for the rest of the week. Cameron had taken out one of the school books Gerard had brought along for him.

"Gerry, what is 25% of 100?" He asked from the back seat.

"25."

"What does point two five mean?"

"Are you studying decimals already?" Gerard asked before he answered the question. For a moment he had forgotten that Cameron's studies were accelerated.

"This section is called percentages, decimals, and fractions." Cameron looked in the rearview mirror at him. "What are they for?"

"I think I'm going to let your tutor tell you all about them later," Gerard said. "I guess in a few days we will have to get back on a schedule of sorts. Maybe we could go away for a long weekend before we do that though. What do you think?"

"Where would we go?"

"Where would you like to go?" Gerard asked as he looked back at him in the mirror and watched a little grin come across his face.

"Can you swim Gerry?"

"I swim pretty well."

"Then can we go to the beach? Mama says I am a good swimmer, but I've never been to the beach."

"Cameron, I don't know if it's warm enough for swimming yet. Perhaps this summer we'll go down to the Caribbean. But maybe we could go to the amusement park down there in Florida."

"Mickey Mouse!" Cameron yelled happily.

"Yes, Mickey Mouse." Gerard smiled when he saw the happiness on his face. He parked in his reserved space. Inside, Glenda was sitting at her desk typing.

"Dr. Wright, I'm so sorry about Ava, what happened?"

"How did you find out?" Gerard asked as he helped Cameron off with his coat.

"The mortician called to let you know that," she looked at Cameron, "everything had been taken care of."

"Oh, of course." Gerard immediately wanted to change the subject.

"Gerry, what is a mortician?"

"It's nothing for you to worry about right now." Gerard cringed. "Glenda, would you order us some lunch?"

"Sure. What would you like?"

"Cameron, what would you like for lunch?" Gerard asked as he watched him climb onto the oversized Italian leather sofa.

"I don't know." Cameron looked around the office. "How long do we have to stay here?"

"Just for a couple of hours," Gerard said apologetically. "I have some meetings and then we'll go. Okay?"

"Let's go play the piano."

"In a few minutes. Let's tell Glenda what we want for lunch."

"I don't want anything to eat. I want to play the piano."

"What about club sandwiches and fruit?" Glenda interrupted with Gerard's usual order from the restaurant across the street.

"That sounds fine, thank you."

"That Steinway is still set up across the lobby," she said from her desk just before she called the order in.

"Come on," Gerard said and took Cameron across the red carpeted lobby to a practice room containing a grand piano. "You can play whatever you like. I'll sit in here with you," he added when he saw the concern in Cameron's eyes.

"Okay." Cameron said and climbed onto the piano bench. "What do you want to hear? I'll play something special for you."

Gerard looked down at the warm grin. "Let me hear the Tchaikovsky again. I love that," he said and right away the room filled with music. He had intentionally left the door open so that anyone in the building would be able to hear. He closed his eyes and listened and even though he knew it was true, he still couldn't believe that a seven year old was the finest pianist he had ever heard.

"Dr. Wright, Cameron, your lunch is here."

"Thanks Glenda." Gerard's dark brown eyes popped open when he heard her voice.

Gerard discovered that the reason why Cameron was not particularly hungry was because he was sleepy. He had his insulin and ate quietly for a while. But when Gerard looked over at the sofa to ask him if he wanted a cookie, his head was against the arm rest and his eyes were closed. Gerard removed his dishes and put his feet up as delicately as he could. He pushed him a little further to the back so if he turned over he wouldn't fall off the couch.

Glenda looked up from her lunch when he came out to her desk. "Can I get you anything?"

"No, go ahead. I don't want to wake him. He's tired."

"How did you get that black eye?"

"Cameron hit me, believe it or not. He was still half asleep."

"What happened last night? Do you want to talk about it?"

"There's not much to add really. Right when we heard the weather sirens last night, we went downstairs. Ava wasn't in her room. I looked for her as much as I could. After the storm, we went to the kitchen and I found her lying in the floor. I thought she had just passed out. She had been sick for a few days. When I touched her—" Gerard's voice broke.

"I'm so sorry."

"There was someone still in the house. He was just a few feet away from Cameron, closer to him than I was." Gerard said softly. "I hadn't told anyone that."

"I understand. I won't say anything." Glenda said. "What are you going to do now?"

"Cameron's doctor told me that he will probably become even more attached to me now, for a little while. He's had to deal with so many losses over the past weeks that he will want to stay close to me."

"To make sure that you don't go away too?"

Gerard nodded. "I'm going to let him stay with me as much as possible, until things calm down. I will have to get some help though."

"Well, why not use the agency that sent Ava?"

"An agency didn't send Ava. I don't know how she happened to find us."

"What do you mean?"

"She wasn't—it's a long story." Gerard fell silent as he looked out the window at the bleak winter sky.

"Why don't I call an agency for you?" Glenda asked as she took out the yellow pages. "You can get the process started before the first of the year." She said as she flipped through the pages.

"Oh." Gerard turned back towards her. "I forgot that tomorrow is New Year's Eve."

"The orchestra party is tomorrow night. I'll make an excuse for you without saying too much."

"Thanks Glenda," he said. He smiled and touched her blonde hair.

"Don't worry about it. Here's the number." She dialed the number and handed him the phone. "Tell them you want someone with excellent local references," she added.

Gerard was on the phone with the placement agency for almost half an hour, but by the time he hung up he was satisfied that they understood what he wanted. Glenda had already shown David into the small meeting room next door since Cameron was still sleeping in his office. Gerard hurried to meet him when he looked at his watch and saw that it was almost 3.

"I'm sorry to keep you waiting," Gerard said coolly. He closed the door behind him, thinking about their blow-up that morning. He could not help but think that soon he would have to find another attorney. Their personal relationship was not going to be enough to overcome their obvious differences.

"I have the document you want," David said and ran his fingers through his blonde hair. "Listen, Gerard I—" David began to speak just before there was a knock at the door

"I'm sorry to disturb you, but Alan Sullivan is here." Glenda said after Gerard opened the door. Alan was standing in the foyer.

"I forgot. Would you ask him to wait please? In one of the other rooms." Gerard thought he saw a look of fear go across Alan's face when he looked in his direction.

"I'll put him somewhere. You've got a full house today."

"If Cameron…"

"I'll watch him."

"What time are they coming, because you'll need two witnesses?" David said and handed him the document to read.

"They should be here any minute, actually," Gerard said as he finished going over the short page that said by signing, the Fuentes agreed not to sue for custody of Cameron. Gerard took his checkbook out of the pocket of his white button-down shirt and began to write.

"That's a lot of money. I just hope that you know what you are doing," David said and shook his head.

Before Gerard could say anything, there was another knock at the door. When he answered it, Glenda, Luis and Alma were standing in the hallway.

"Come in." Gerard stepped aside. This small conference room was designed for two or three people, not five. "Glenda, would you mind staying a moment to witness something?"

"Yes, Dr. Wright."

"This is the document we talked about earlier," Gerard said and Luis and Alma read over it quickly.

"You got the check ready?" Luis asked, placing a brown leather briefcase on the chair next to Gerard.

"Yes, it's right here."

"That's some of Leon's papers and things, some music he wrote and a journal," Luis said. "I wouldn't read it out loud, if you know what I mean. Some of it's not G-rated."

"I thought all his things were in storage," Gerard said, frowning at the bag.

"Well, this was at my mother's house. I don't know how it got there. You might just throw the diary away, but I guess the music belongs to the kid. It might be worth something," Luis said with his usual air of nonchalance.

Gerard sighed and handed him the check after everyone there had signed the document. Glenda left after witnessing the signatures.

"Do you think that we could come and visit Cameron sometimes?" Alma asked. Her eyes were sincere when she looked at Gerard.

"Mrs. Fuentes," David began.

"I was his babysitter a long time ago."

"I suppose it would be all right if Cameron wants to see you," Gerard answered. She began to smile.

"Well, it's been a pleasure doing business with you," Luis said as he folded the check and put it in his wallet. "Come on Alma, let's go."

"I better be going too, Gerard," David said as soon as they were alone in the room.

"Thank you for coming David," Gerard said.

Gerard waited for David to leave before he opened the leather briefcase. His heart was pounding in his chest as he touched the small blue book. He took his hand away from it when he saw how he was shaking. Why was he so afraid of a book? He chastised himself, but then he admitted to himself what he was afraid of: perhaps the book talked about how Cameron was treated. Gerard knew that he could hardly bear to know any more details about the cruelty Leon had subjected the child to. Gerard had already made up his mind that Leon de la Valle was an animal, an insane, inhumane beast of the most evil sort.

Gerard put the book back in the bag and carried it with him when he went to talk with Alan. The door to his office was still closed and Glenda pointed to the room where Alan was waiting for him. He did not get up, but held out a slender hand.

"Hello Gerard."

"Hello Alan. I must apologize for keeping you waiting like this. It's been kind of hectic this afternoon." Gerard shook his cold hand.

"I can see that you're—" Alan froze for a moment.

"What's the matter?" Gerard looked in the direction that held Alan's attention.

"That, that bag looked familiar," Alan said. He shrugged and shifted in his chair. "I thought it was mine for a moment."

"It's some things I have to go through later on. What did you want to see me about?"

"Well, the thing is, I need a job. These odd gigs aren't keeping the rent paid." He took a pack of Marlboro cigarettes out of his pocket and lit one with an ornate silver lighter that did not look like it belonged to a man with financial troubles. "I have the background to play any kind of music, but then, you already know that."

"Of course," Gerard said. He sat back to avoid a little of the smoke. "I don't know if I have anything available right now. I'd have to look over the roster."

"Anything you could do would be greatly appreciated."

"There's something I've wanted to ask you Alan," Gerard said and stared straight into his eyes.

"What is that?"

"Why is Cameron afraid of you?" Gerard waited, but got no answer. He thought back to the trip he and Cameron made to the mall for Christmas shopping and how Cameron had reacted when he saw Alan in the toy store. He felt himself growing angrier by the minute. "Did you see Cameron the night his father took him?"

"I was in and out that night. I can't remember," Alan said smugly.

"If I find out that you hurt that child, I'll kill you," Gerard said. He used all his restraint to keep his voice down.

"I don't know what you're talking about."

"Maybe until we clear things up and you get your memory back, you better not come around anymore."

"Well, sure if that's the way you want it." Alan walked out and left the door open behind him.

Gerard sat there alone for several minutes after Alan left. He shook his head as he looked at the worn, brown leather bag on the floor and reached down to pick it up. The small blue book mesmerized him and he opened it to the first page.

I don't know how to tell Maggie what I've done.

Gerard's hands trembled as he read.

I didn't mean to hurt him, not like that. It was one of them, one of the others inside me that did it. I wouldn't do that to my own boy, not the way my father did it to me. I could see it happening, but I couldn't stop it. Oh God, what if he tells her? I stole this book from the drugstore today. The girl behind the counter was looking right at me, and just smiled when I put it in my pocket. That's the way it always is with girls, guys too, I guess. I told B that I wasn't like that and he said it didn't matter, that I might like it anyway. I guess he was right. But I like this leather jacket he bought me even better. He is in love with me. That's why he brought me the other stuff too. It's the only thing that makes the voices stop. Maggie is so stupid. She caught me in the bathroom and said she'd put me out if I took anymore. She just didn't get it that it's the only thing keeping me from killing her like they told me. I love Maggie. I don't want to hurt her. I didn't even mean to hurt Cameron just now. I'm so sorry. I can hear him under the bed crying. If he doesn't shut up I'm going to

The entry stopped there. Gerard felt nauseous when he thought about how it must have ended. The next page was dated October 31st.

B has gone crazy. He bought me this damned pager, and he calls me every hour. He'll keep paging until I call back too. He wants to get together tonight. I'm playing at his party and then he wants to meet me at the apartment later. I wonder what he tells his wife when he's out with me. Maybe she doesn't care. Maggie would leave me if she found out. I love her. The others don't. They hate her and wish she was dead, but she's mine and I want her. I've wanted her since the first time I saw her singing at that bar. It was good then. I was okay for awhile after I got out of the hospital. No one knew. I guess I should have gone back to the doctor when the voices started up again. It's too late now. There goes the pager again. It was Alan this time. He's always pestering me about those damn songs. What's it to him anyway? They're mine. I'll have to see him tonight at our gig, but I'm going to get out of there quick after it's over. Maggie knows I hit Cameron, but she doesn't know anything else. I don't think he told her. She screamed and cried and even punched me. It hurt more than I thought it would and I got mad and slapped her down. She didn't fight me anymore after that. I'm going to clear out of here for awhile before she goes off again. I'll go over to the apartment. B rented the place so he wouldn't be seen going to hotels all over town. He was so happy that first night there that he bought me a closet full of clothes, Gucci and Armani, the stuff I like that he wears. I hate this dump. I bet if I asked I could just move into the apartment for good. I don't know what I'd do with Maggie and Cameron. Sometimes I think about smothering them both while they're sleeping, but I know that's just one of the voices telling me to do that. Maggie has been taking Cameron with her to work at the conductor's house. He thinks he's so great. If I find out there's something with him and Maggie I'll kill him too. I know he doesn't remember me. I've got more talent in one finger than he has in his whole body and yet he's supposed to know so much. But why can't I play like I used to? People think I'm good, but I'm nothing like before. It all started to go away when he was born. Cameron is taking away my music. I don't know how he's doing it, but I've got to stop him. I took him to the studio and made him play for me. My God, he sounds just like me. I've got to find out what he's doing to me. I got this book because I thought it might help if I wrote it down. That's what they said at the hospital. But this book is not helping. I'm going to call B and tell him to meet me at the apartment now. I need something to get me through this gig, and I need it right now.

Gerard looked away from the page for a moment. He only remembered seeing Leon once or twice and then only briefly. He wondered who had been telling Leon so much about him, and he wondered who the initial "B" belonged to. It was almost 4 and he and Cameron should be leaving, but he decided to read another page. The next entry was several days later.

I'm going to kill Alan. I can't believe that bastard thought he could do this to me and get away with it. He's all washed up. He's been in and out of the hospital as many times as I have and he hasn't been able to write anything in years. So he stole my song and put his name on it. Did he really think I wouldn't recognize my own music? He's been lying to me all along. He said the music I wrote was just "okay" and

> *that the music company had turned them all down. I've been living in poverty for years because I couldn't make a living and now I find out that he sold "Passion Flowers" to the record company with his name on it! I found the check stub and a letter in his desk drawer. The letter from the record company guy said it was the best modern jazz composition he had heard in years and that Alan was a genius and they would look forward to recording more of his songs. His songs? Alan a genius? I'm the genius then because I wrote it! All these years I've thought I was a failure, just like my father said I would be, and now this. I won't let him get away with this. No wonder he has always stuck so close to me. He offered to give me all the money if I didn't file a lawsuit. Of course, I'm going to take the money and then I'm going to sue him and everyone will know my work and that he is a fraud. I'm sure B can handle the case. I hate Alan and I told him I wouldn't be playing music with him anymore. I don't care if he does have a lot of gigs lined up. He was so desperate that night that he even tried to seduce me. I laughed at him and told him how pathetic he was afterwards. He cried like a baby.*

Gerard straightened in his chair and turned the page. The handwriting was beginning to look different by the next paragraph, which was not dated.

> *Why won't she leave me alone? I didn't mean to hit her that hard. She hit her head. What if I've killed her? I just wanted to see her, to talk to her and tell her about the song and the money. But she did not want me there. Then Cameron woke up crying. I just wanted him to be quiet. I don't know why I did it, but after she fell and was just lying there in the floor. I*

> *grabbed Cameron. I shouldn't have done that. I should have just left him there. I didn't mean to do this. As soon as we got here, they started talking to me. They told me that he had stolen my gifts and that he was evil. They were all talking at once, telling me what to do. They were telling me how to put an end to this evil child. I had to tie him up because he wouldn't stop fighting. He was only crying at first, but I had to put the gag over his mouth so no one could hear him screaming. He was always so loud. I got scared when B walked in, but he helped me. I told Maggie I should never have children, that she should get rid of it. But she wouldn't listen. Cameron should never have been born. She thought I was afraid he might be like me and have to go in the hospital all the time, but that wasn't it. I knew from the day she first told me she was pregnant with him that he was going to destroy me if I didn't destroy him first. It's just that he's so quiet now. When I look at him, I feel sorry. I don't think he's breathing. I can't leave him here in the apartment for just anyone to find. I'll take him to church.*

Gerard slammed the book shut. He never wanted to see the horrible thing again. But even as he put it back in the bag, he knew he had learned something more. There was someone else there the night Cameron was taken and it wasn't Alan. It was this "B." He was the threat the doctor had mentioned. Gerard expected to see Cameron talking to Glenda when he walked back around front, but she was at her desk and his office door was still closed.

"He hasn't come out yet?"

"No, it's been quiet the whole time," Glenda said.

"Did you lock the door?" Gerard asked after he tried the knob and it did not turn.

"No, maybe it was already set to lock when you shut it."

"I don't even have the keys."

"Don't worry. I have a set right here." Glenda rummaged through her desk drawer and a handed a small silver key to Gerard. He opened the door quietly so as not to startle Cameron awake. At first glance the room looked just the way he had left it. Then Gerard's heart stopped. The window that he never used was open, and Cameron was gone.

Chapter Eleven

"Cameron! Cameron!" Gerard frantically opened the closet doors as he prayed that he was only hiding.

"Gerard, what's the—" Glenda came in behind him.

"He's gone. Oh my God, he's gone." Gerard raced out of the office. "Call the police." He yelled back over his shoulder as he ran through the darkened theater. He threw on the lights and called out to Cameron, hoping he would pop up from one of the 1,800 seats inside and say that this was all a joke. But no one called back to him as he stood on the stage. He began his search of the practice rooms, but inside he already knew that Cameron was not there. He just did not know who had taken him. It had to be someone who came there this afternoon, he thought. All of the people he suspected were equally dangerous.

Gerard heard sirens and ran back to the front of the building.

"Did you find him?" Glenda asked.

Gerard shook his head as he went out to meet the police.

"Did you call about a missing child?"

"Yes. He's my ward. His name is Cameron. He was sleeping in my office and when I went back to check on him, he was gone." Gerard spoke quickly as they walked back inside.

"Have you searched the building?" the red-haired policewoman asked as she looked around the huge structure. "There are a lot of places to hide in a place like this."

"I was just doing that. But he wouldn't—"

"We'll get some back-up to help us cover the area. How old is he?"

"Seven. He's a diabetic," Gerard said. "He can't survive without his insulin."

"We're going to do everything we can to find him," she said. Gerard had not noticed that her partner was on his radio while they were talking.

"Two other units are on the way. I'll start searching, if you want to get a statement from him," her partner said as he started down the hall.

"Where exactly was the child, sir?"

"He was in my office." Gerard led her to the side where the offices were. "He was taking a nap."

"Do you normally come here at this time every day?"

"No, I've been away with the holidays and other things."

"Has anyone been here today? Anyone at all, deliveries?"

"There have been a lot of people here today. That's why we came over. I had to meet with some people. There was Luis and Alma Fuentes, Alan Sullivan, and my lawyer was even here for a few minutes."

"Was Cameron with you then?"

"No, he was taking a nap in my office. We got here a little after 12:30. Glenda was here and we ordered lunch from the deli next door. It was getting close to the time for my appointment when I noticed Cameron was sleeping, so I came out and left him there on the couch." Gerard's eyes filled with tears.

"Did you lock the door?"

"No, that was strange. I thought it must have gotten into the locked position by accident. My secretary had keys. I couldn't find mine."

"What time did you see him last?"

"When I closed the door, just before 3 o'clock." Gerard stopped when a voice came over her radio.

"Backup is outside. Tell them to start upstairs. I've gone through the rooms downstairs. I took a look outside the office and there are definite shoe prints below the window," the policeman said and paused. "I think we've got some blood here. This looks bad."

Gerard pushed open the door to his office so he could see the man on the radio. He was dark, heavyset, and looked about 30. He eyed Gerard closely for a moment. "I'm sorry. I didn't realize you were right there. Don't touch anything else until we can get the lab guys in here."

"Dr. Wright, this can't be happening," Glenda said as she started to cry.

"Glenda, please don't." Gerard took a deep breath. "Maybe if I went around to some of the neighboring businesses…"

"Two other officers are doing that," she said and talked into her radio again. Her partner joined them in the hallway.

"Dr. Wright, we're treating this as a kidnapping. The best thing for you to do is go home and wait for a phone call. Ransom demands are usually made within 24 hours."

"But…"

"The detectives will meet you there in a few minutes. They'll alert the FBI."

Gerard agreed with them, even though he felt he should stay and canvass the neighborhood. He gathered his things out of habit. He tucked the brown leather briefcase under his arm and picked up Cameron's jacket. He squeezed the jacket to his chest. "Just hold on baby. I'll find you," he said to the air.

Glenda was waiting by her desk and they walked out together. "Do you want me to drive you?"

"No, I'm all right to drive. You go on home. I'll try to let you know what's happening."

"I'll wait to hear from you," she said and hugged him. "He's going to be fine. I know it."

"Thanks." Gerard got into the black Mercedes and made his way home.

The house was quiet when Gerard went inside. He had never realized how much he looked forward to Cameron's exuberant greetings. He stood in the foyer and waited to hear the little footsteps running toward him, but they never came. He dropped the bag and his jacket into a chair in the den and headed straight for the bar. "I need a drink." He thought. He reached into the cabinet and took out a new bottle of whiskey. He got a tumbler out and decided to skip the ice. He poured himself what had to be a triple and put the glass to his lips. He knew this would take the edge off and make the days' events not hurt so much. He caught sight of his reflection in the mirror behind the bar just as he was about to take the first swallow. He froze. This was not what Cameron needed. He did not need a drink, he thought. He needed to be rational and sober to find this little boy who was depending on him. He may be Cameron's only hope and he was not going to waste it.

Gerard poured the whiskey in the glass down the sink at the bar. He looked at the bottle, and did the same with it. He dropped the other unopened bottles into the trash, just as the phone rang. He rushed to it and picked up before the second ring. "Hello?"

There was no answer.

"Hello?" Gerard's hand was shaking as he held the phone. Still, the line was silent.

"If you'd like to make a call, please hang up and try again." The automated recording said over the sound of the dial tone.

Gerard frowned at the phone as he hung it up, praying it would ring again. He almost jumped out of his skin when he heard the loud knock at the door.

"Detective Fisher, what are you doing here?" Gerard knew that he did not need a homicide detective.

"I heard the call come in. I recognized the address," Fisher said. He and two other detectives carrying cases entered the house. "This is Detective Armstrong and Detective Fox. They'll be handling the case for now."

Gerard shook their hands briefly.

"What happened?" Fisher asked.

"Well, the phone rang just now, but no one said anything. Maybe it was..."

"Let us get set up in case they call again. That was quick." Armstrong went past them and into the den with the equipment to monitor the phone.

"Are you crazy? We can't tell him what we saw. I don't want the police around asking me questions. Don't you remember why?" Luis yelled after he snatched the phone away from Alma.

"Of course I remember. We could make an anonymous call. We have to do something." Alma knew she would never forget this afternoon. It had started out a happy day. The money was one thing, but she was actually happier that this Dr. Wright had agreed to let her see Cameron sometimes. Luis was not a good man, but he was good to her, and she loved him. But she knew that he would never really understand the sense of loss she'd felt after she was attacked that night in her dressing room before the show. He viewed the fact that she would never be able to have children as meaning that it would always be just the two of them.

Alma remembered that after they had left the theater, Luis parked around the corner and reached into his jacket pocket. "Would you look at that, baby? That's $50,000 with our names on it." Luis' blue eyes were sparkling with happiness.

"That's more money than I've ever seen in my life."

"Let's go to the bank and cash it. Then let's go—"

"Luis, look there's David." Alma pointed to the silver Porsche parked at the stop sign beside them. David did not look over at them in the few seconds that he was there. But a flicker of movement in the back of the car caught her eye. She looked closer and saw a tiny arm sticking out from under a dark green blanket. "What on earth?"

"What is it?" Luis asked after the car had turned the corner.

"Follow him."

"What for? We're on our way to the bank remember? I don't want to talk to or see David Boudreau ever again."

"Follow him, Luis." Alma grabbed his arm and he obeyed. "This can't be right, but I think he has Cameron." She frowned as they picked up speed.

"I don't see him, wait, there he is." Luis maneuvered to the lane that David's car was in. "You really think he's taken Cameron? Maybe Wright told him he could."

"I don't think he'd be covered up in the back seat like that. Get over; he's getting on the interstate."

Luis tried to keep far enough back from David so that he wouldn't recognize them. They drove behind him for 30 minutes, away from the city of New Orleans, towards the area known as the north shore. They rode in silence until they approached the six-mile bridge. "Should we keep going or turn back?"

"I don't know where he could be going."

"A lot of those rich people have houses on the water over here." Luis said as a light rain began to splatter against the windshield. "We'll keep going a little farther. Alma, are you sure you saw something?"

Alma did not answer as quickly as she should have. "It looked like a child's arm coming from under a blanket." She was saying just as blue lights began to flash behind them. "Oh no, what is this?"

"Damn it." Luis said under his breath as he pulled over and watched the silver Porsche's tail lights fade out of sight.

"Good evening folks. I need your license and registration. You passed me doing 78," the female officer said as she came to the driver's side door

"I'm sorry, officer. I didn't realize we were going that fast. I was trying to get her to a job interview on time." Luis smiled his most charming smile.

She looked at him, and then at his license. She paused a moment before she told him, "I'm going to let you go with a warning this time, but slow it down."

"Thank you. I certainly will." Luis took back his identification.

"That was close," Alma said after the policewoman had gotten back into her squad car. "I'm glad she just gave you a warning."

"I've had enough of this for one day Alma. Let's go back. We've lost him anyway."

"But Luis, what are we going to do?"

He tried to think of a way to placate her before she got even more upset. "We're not even sure of anything right now. Let's make sure there's even any danger. If there is, we'll do something then." Luis lied. He didn't have any intention of getting involved in anything, dangerous or otherwise. He had a feeling that he already knew why David wanted to get his hands on the kid so bad. Cameron must know something pretty bad about him, like what happened the night his father died, Luis thought as they drove back to New Orleans. Luis decided that it was none of his business. He had $50,000 and was moving to Miami, and that was all he cared about.

"It's just a little farther now. I can do this." David thought. "I'll just wait until it gets late and then I'll take him out to the lake." Sweat beaded up on his forehead even though it was 45 degrees outside and raining. "How could I be so stupid?" He slapped himself on the forehead. Taking the child had not been part of the plan. It was just an impulse to put a stop to the threat of him telling Gerard one day. There would have been so many easier ways for the boy to have an "accident." But he couldn't think about that now. He had taken one step, now he would have to take another.

David drove east along Interstate 10 until he reached the exit for his fishing cabin at the lake. He had given Cameron an injection of Valium out of his own stash before he took him so that he wouldn't wake up while they were traveling. "Maybe I gave him too much," he thought. He hoped he had. He never wanted to look into those damned eyes again anyway. There was something about the way Cameron looked at him that made him feel like the kid could see right through him. He did not like it at all.

He glanced in the rearview mirror as he made the turn onto his property and drove towards the stilted cabin that had been in his family for years. The hurricane season almost washed it away every year lately, but he kept getting it repaired. His wife thought it was for sentimental reasons, but he liked having a place that was remote where he could be alone, or even better, be with a friend.

The dusk-to-dawn lights that he'd installed were already on when he pulled into the driveway. He would have preferred darkness. He turned off the ignition and took a deep breath. It was still too early to get rid of him. He would have to take the child into the house and wait a couple of hours. David decided it would speed things up if he unlocked the front door first, so he found his door keys and got out.

"Well, hello Mr. Boudreau, I wasn't expecting to see you tonight," a voice said from behind David. Ben Warren, his caretaker smiled a toothy grin.

"Oh Ben," David said, almost jumping out of his skin. "I didn't know you were here. You startled me." He tried to explain his fearful expression.

"I just brought by a load of wood. I didn't know how soon you would be using the cabin again."

"Oh, I was just checking to see if things were in shape to bring the family out this weekend." David's face drained completely white when he saw the small tennis shoe poking out from under the blanket in the backseat. If he could see it, what could Ben see? His eyes were over 60 years old and it was dark. Surely, he couldn't see anything.

"This weekend? Won't you and your family still be having your big New Year's celebration?" Ben frowned. "Are you feeling all right? You don't look too good."

David's face flushed with embarrassment at having told such an obvious lie. His weekend celebration at New Year's was one of the biggest parties of the social season. "I've had that flu that's been going around. First it was the kids, then my wife, now I guess it's my turn." David tried to smile. "Well, I meant next weekend. I happened to be out this way visiting a client and thought I would stop in and have a look around."

"Well. That's good then. I can show you some of the new work I did out there on the deck and in the kitchen." Ben looked at the car. "Is that a new car?"

"No." David instinctively moved to block his view in the window.

"It looks different I guess. It sure is a beauty, though."

"Thanks Ben." David realized that he was not going to be able to get out of this little tour. His best bet was to try to get it over with quickly. "Come on; let's go have a look at that deck before it starts to rain again."

"Sure." Ben smiled at him and glanced back over his shoulder at the car before they walked around to the back of the house.

"It's him. He said he would be back for me and he did," Cameron thought as he listened to the sound of voices, one of them was familiar to him. He recognized it immediately and was filled with terror. The voices got quieter and then seemed to fade away. Cameron pulled the heavy blanket from over his face only to discover he was still in darkness. The sun had set since he closed his eyes in Gerry's office. He inched up in the back seat and looked around. It didn't take him but a second to realize that he was somewhere he had been before, somewhere very far from home.

He slid out of the backseat and out of the car. He made sure to close the car door softly so that it barely made a "click" after he got out. Cameron ran for the woods that surrounded the property in a blind panic. It was getting very dark, but it didn't matter. All he knew was that he had to get away from him.

He was so frightened that he wouldn't even let himself think of his name. It was so horrible that last time when he had found him alone after his father had gone out that Cameron never wanted to go through that again. He knew about death and about dying. As he ran, he decided that he would rather die than live through another night like that. When he awakened the next day, he was in the hospital. His mother was there and so was Gerard.

"Where's Gerry?" Cameron thought. His arm hurt and he stopped and looked down at it once he was sheltered by the trees. There was blood on the sleeve of his blue shirt. He touched the spot where it hurt the most and could tell he had been stuck with a needle there. His insulin injections never hurt like that though. "I just want to go home. I just want to go back to Gerry and Mama." He cried silently as the thoughts ran through his mind. "What if I never get home again?" Cameron sat down beside a tree. He could see lights on in the cabin, but he didn't see anyone. He shook his head as he looked around at the trees and knew that he would be easily seen there. He started running again, looking for a place to hide.

"Dr. Wright, we've got everything all set up in the den for whenever the call comes," said Detective Diane Gray, nodding towards the phone surveillance equipment.

"Good." Gerard looked up from the spot he'd been staring at on the floor, thinking.

"We need to ask you some more questions. The more we know..."

"Anything you want to know."

"Cameron is your ward. How did he come to live with you?"

"He's my housekeeper's son, Magdalene de la Valle."

"The de la Valle murder case?"

"Yes, that's the one. She asked me to keep him. We're just learning to be a family, and now—" He could not continue.

"Do you have any enemies, someone with a grudge?"

"None that I know of, except..." Gerard hesitated. He had to be careful about what he said. "Cameron was being abused."

"That was the wife's motive, wasn't it?"

"I've been taking Cameron to see a psychologist and it seems..."

"What is it Dr. Wright?" she asked softly.

"There was someone else involved in the abuse. Cameron hasn't said so directly. But it was a tall blonde man and I think his name is Alan Sullivan," said Gerard. It suddenly occurred to him where he should be looking. He sprang out of his chair.

"Wait a minute, wait a minute. Let us talk to him. Do you have his address?"

Gerard stopped when she put her hand on his arm. "No, but I have his phone number." He quickly got his address book out and gave her the number he'd written down for Alan.

"I'll trace it," she said and typed the number into the laptop computer on the coffee table. In a matter of minutes, she yelled an address to her partner, and she and Fisher were on their way out the door, leaving him in the company of two other officers.

The clock ticked away each agonizing second as Gerard waited for the phone to ring. He got up and went to the den doorway. "I'll just be upstairs for a few minutes. There's a phone in my bedroom," he said to the officers on his way upstairs.

As soon as he closed the bedroom door behind him, he went to his window. He hadn't done it in years, but the climb down the fire escape ladder was as easy as he remembered. The ladder dropped off out of sight of the front of the house so he did not have to worry about the police seeing him leave by the driveway at the back of his property. There was no way that he was going to miss hearing what Alan had to say.

He drove to the address he heard the police say and saw them at the door of the motel-style apartment. Gerard parked down the block on the other side of the street and watched the two detectives knock and wait, but when there was no answer they went back to their car.

Gerard did not have to wait half an hour after the detectives drove away, to see Alan come home. He only gave him time to shut his front door before he got out of his car and ran down the street to Alan's door. His knock was answered right away.

"Gerard, this is a surprise. I didn't think—" Alan began.

"Where is he?" Gerard pushed Alan against the wall and his hands were at his throat before he realized what he was doing. "Tell me where he is!"

Alan pushed Gerard and he fell back against the front door, finally closing it. Gerard sprang up from the floor and landed a punch in the center of Alan's stomach, knocking the air out of him. "What the hell is wrong with you?" asked Alan when he was able to speak. Gerard stood looking at him.

"What have you done with Cameron?"

"What do you mean?" Alan stood up, frowning. "We can fight if you want, but wouldn't it be better if you just told me what was going on?"

"Cameron is missing. It just happened this afternoon. I've already sent the police over here. I'm sure they'll be back soon. Tell me what you know about this or I'll have to start letting some people know about what I've read in Leon's diary. It's a matter of theft."

"All right, I'll talk to you, but I didn't take the boy. You're pointing the police in the wrong direction."

"Whoever has taken him had something to do with Leon's murder. It's got to be something to do with that." Gerard ran his hand through his black hair and shook his head.

"I didn't kill Leon. I tried, but Magdalene beat me to it." Alan walked into his living room and Gerard followed. He took a bottle of whiskey from the mantle. "Want a drink?"

"No. What do you mean you tried?"

Alan did not answer for a moment and then took a long drink from the bottle. "I guess I messed that up, too. I do that sometimes," he said, his voice cold. "I don't know what you read in his diary. He could be such a..." He took another drink. "We used to hang out together after the group broke up. We would party together. He found out about the songs and I had to stop him. If things go well, I'll be rich."

"With stolen music?" Gerard couldn't help but ask.

"He was a genius with music. I've never seen anything like it, except when I hear the kid play the piano." He took a sip this time. "The night he died, Leon had been with me over at the motel. He knew I always had some drugs for him. This time I slipped a little something extra into his." Alan's blonde hair drooped across his forehead. "I thought it would've killed him right away, but it didn't. I didn't know what to do. He started asking for a drink so I went down to the corner to buy a bottle. I hoped it would be over by the time I got back." His voice got lower. "Only when I got back, he was gone. I was so scared that, now that he was loaded, he'd start talking about the music. I went out to look for him. I went to his place and looked in the window, and there he was talking to Cameron."

Gerard's heart stopped. No one could know Cameron's secret. "What did you see?"

"They were just in the kitchen. I figured that if he was at home, he wouldn't go out to the club and talk to that music producer before the poison took effect. So, I decided to just wait in my car for awhile and see if anything happened. I watched that apartment for almost an hour." Alan looked Gerard in the eye. "I saw everything and I know who killed Leon."

Chapter Twelve

"What do you mean?" Gerard's blood went cold, but he tried to show no expression on his face. Cameron's secret had to stay safe.

"I told you I was outside." Alan looked him in the eye. "I know Magdalene didn't kill Leon, but what I can't figure out is why she would take the blame for him." Alan lit a cigarette. "I mean, what is he to her?"

"I don't understand." said Gerard. The room seemed to grow warmer. "Of course she would protect him, he's her…" He stopped at the moment he realized that they were not talking about the same person. Gerard got a mental picture of the other tall, blonde man that he knew, the man in the picture Cameron drew. He looked Alan in the eye and he nodded. "But that's impossible."

"It's possible all right. Your lawyer gets around. I guess he has a kind of double life," Alan said. "But then, you already know that, don't you?"

Gerard shook his head. "I never—it was never like that with us. Why didn't you go to the police?"

"And tell them what, that I was trying to kill a man, but someone beat me to it? I figured you had decided together that she would take the blame," he said and paused. "For some reason."

"That's not the way it happened. I didn't know." The words made his throat throb. He stood up. "I've got to go. I have to find them. Do you know where he would go?"

"No." Alan followed him to the door. "I know you won't believe it, but I never touched the kid. That's not my thing. Maybe, I did do those other things, but not that." He took a deep breath. "David is sick and Leon was sick in a different way. He heard voices and stuff." Alan tried to look sincere. He didn't want him to mention his name when he talked to the police. If the investigation was reopened, someone might ask about the girl, Ava. At that moment, he thought about leaving town, but knew that would probably only make him look more guilty.

"I know." Gerard thought about the diary as he ran back to his car. He knew the police must have missed him by now. They may be looking for him since they had told him to stay put. He drove towards his house anyway. He couldn't help but realize that he did not know where to look. He picked up his car phone and dialed a familiar number. There was no answer on David's private line. His home number was answered on the second ring.

"Boudreau residence."

"May I speak to Mr. Boudreau please?" Gerard recognized the housekeeper's voice.

"He's not here, may I take a message?"

"Is Mrs. Boudreau at home?" Gerard tried not to sound impatient, and wondered what he was going to say to her.

"Hello, this is Susan Boudreau."

"Susan, this is Gerard Wright. I was looking for David." He tried to sound casual.

"He hasn't made it home yet. I'm sure he'll be here soon, though. We're meeting my parents for dinner. I can give him a message for you."

"Would you just ask him to call me later?"

"Of course I will."

"Thanks." Gerard hung up. Susan was the perfect wife. She was the daughter of a senator, involved in dozens of charities, and from one of the wealthiest families in the state. You couldn't open the newspaper without seeing her, and David, on the society page. What would she do when she found out who her husband really was?

"It's okay Luis, you're right." Alma knew there was no point in arguing with him. He was never going to get involved, especially now that they had the money.

"I'm glad you're coming around," said Luis, as he leaned down and kissed her lips. "Why don't we go out to dinner and celebrate? Tomorrow we can make our plane reservations for Miami."

"Right." Alma lingered in his arms. "You go ahead and get ready. I think I'd like to go to Martine's."

"Excellent choice." Luis smiled and headed down the hallway to their bedroom.

Alma didn't leave until she heard the shower come on. She knew Luis would look for her, and that he would be angry, but there was something wrong and she had to try to help Cameron. She could remember holding him in her arms and giving him a bottle when he was only a few months old. He had the most beautiful green eyes that she had ever seen, just like his father.

She thought back about those days as she drove to Gerard's mansion. It didn't seem like it was only six years ago. Her life had changed so much since the attack. For a while afterwards, she'd wished they had just killed her instead of raping, strangling, and leaving her for dead in her dressing room before what would have been the most important night of her life. There had been a record producer in the audience. "Big deal," she thought out loud. "No one was there to help me when I needed it."

She shook her head as she turned onto the street with all the beautiful, historic houses. Maybe no one had helped her, but she was going to do whatever she could to help Cameron.

Gerard took a deep breath when he turned on to his street. He was not prepared for the police reprimand that he was sure he would receive. Just before he was about to turn into the driveway, he saw the black Nissan come around the corner in the opposite direction.

He stopped and Alma Fuentes got out. He opened his car door and stepped out before she walked up to the house.

"Mrs. Fuentes, what are you doing here?"

"Dr. Wright, I was just looking for you. I see all these police cars."

"Cameron's missing. Here, get in for a minute," said Gerard, motioning for her to get into the car. He backed up a few yards, out of sight of the police in the living room.

"I just came to tell you about this afternoon."

"If it's about the money—"

"No, I saw David this afternoon and I thought I saw a child in the backseat. It must have been Cameron."

"Well, why didn't you tell the police?"

"We knew David from before. He paid us to ask for custody of Cameron. I don't know why," she said. "We have had trouble with the police before and Luis didn't want to call them, but I had to tell you." She blinked and tears fell from her eyes. "I wanted the money, but I would never want anything to happen to the baby. I'm sorry."

"I understand. Alma, did you see where they went?"

"We followed the car for a little while. He went to the north shore, but we couldn't follow him past the bridge."

"Okay, thanks Alma. I know David has a cabin over there, but I can't remember where. I'll find it though." He squeezed her hand for a second before she got out. "Thank you. Go on home and I'll call you when he's been found."

"All right." Alma nodded, but knew that she was not going home to Luis, or to Miami.

David stood beside his car as Ben backed his black Ford F-150 out of the driveway. He waved goodbye to him and waited for the red tail lights to disappear. He opened the car door and threw back the heavy green blanket. To his horror, there was no one there. The car was empty. "No!" he screamed, and then stopped himself. "All I need to do is call more attention out here," he thought. He shut the door hoping that no one had just heard his outburst.

David quickly surveyed the area. Going to the left, led straight to the woods. It was dark and cold; surely the child wouldn't go in there. To the right, down the driveway, was the road. Cameron could be down there now, walking until a car stopped to pick him up, thought David as he raced towards the road.

The dirt road was soft beneath his feet. With each step he ran, he felt himself sink a little deeper. When David reached the road illuminated only by street lights, he looked for signs of movement. There was nothing. In the winter season, the area was only sparsely populated with fishermen. Most of the cabins were dark on either side of the road. David looked frantically through the yards on the darkened street until he saw a car coming. He darted behind the bushes and waited until it passed before he stepped out again.

He realized that he had walked far enough that he should have seen some sign of Cameron if he was on this road. David cursed out loud and headed back the way he had come. This was not something that he was looking forward to doing. He did not want to kill him, but he was left with no choice.

It was just a matter of time before the child remembered everything. Even if he could convince everyone that the kid was crazy, just the scandal of being accused of these things would ruin his political career. He could never let that happen. He was going to stop everything that had gotten him into this mess: the drugs and the parties that had gotten completely out of hand. Now it seemed he couldn't feel anything anymore, and it just took more and more to stimulate him.

It must just be the drugs, he thought. That had to be the first thing to go. He would really tone down his behavior, but first he had this kid to take care of. He thought to himself that it was really too bad that he couldn't have a little more fun with him before he did it, but there was no time for that now. He ran back towards his house.

Cameron could see the moon through the boards of the abandoned boat shed. It was wet on the inside and muddy. He was afraid to look around and see what other things might be in there with him, but he had to do it. Snakes scared him, but then so did crawfish. He was sure that there were plenty of both inside there with him. He was right. The little crawfish, mudbugs as some called them, seemed to be forming a circle around him. They were crawling up through the rickety floorboards. He put his hand over his mouth to keep his scream inside. He crawled to the side of the shed and got as close to the wall as he could.

"Please come for me Gerry," he thought. Then he heard the footsteps right beside the shed. There was nowhere else to run and Cameron sat there motionless. "Maybe he won't look in here." His heart was pounding in his chest and he had the sick, lightheaded feeling that he got when he didn't have his insulin at the right time. The doorway of the shed began to sway, and he kept his eyes fixed on it. He didn't hear the footsteps anymore and began to breathe again, when suddenly the moonlight was blocked out. Cameron felt strong hands lift him off the ground.

"Be quiet, kid," a voice he did not recognize whispered to him. Cameron looked into the face of the stranger. The gray haired man stepped out of the shed carrying him and looked around the darkened woods. "I don't know what the hell is going on, but I'm taking you out of here." He looked at him. "You're okay now; I'm not going to hurt you," he said as he walked quickly towards the edge of the woods. Cameron could see a pickup truck parked in the driveway, and the old man seemed to run faster the closer they got to it.

"What are you doing, Ben?" David asked from the other side of the truck.

"Well, sir I could ask you that same thing." He held tightly to Cameron.

"Stay out of this, it doesn't concern you." David wiped the sweat from his forehead and took a deep breath of the cold air.

The temperature had dropped so much that Cameron could see his breath as a mist in the night air. He turned his face away from David.

He didn't want to see him again or remember any of it.

"I don't know what's happening here, and maybe I am just the caretaker, but I know that he doesn't belong here with you. I'm going to take him home." Ben did not move an inch when David walked towards him.

"I can't let you do that." David said, his voice cold, just as he took the small handgun out of the pocket of his tan overcoat. "Put him down." David waited while Ben set Cameron down, his eye on the gun every second.

"Run." Ben whispered. He lunged at David and got his hands on the gun. He knew that he was no match for the younger, stronger man. He began to struggle with him for the gun. A few seconds later it went off.

Cameron was just at the back of the house and turned around. He screamed when he saw Ben tumble to the ground and David start walking towards him.

Ben rolled over onto his side and dragged himself to the open door of his truck. His side was bleeding and he had almost forgotten how bad a gunshot hurt, it had been so many years since the war. He reached inside his truck and took out his shotgun. Just before David got out of his sight, he fired.

Gerard sped away without waiting for Alma to get back in her car. The north shore was 45 minutes away, but at the speed he was going he could make it a lot faster than that. By the time he got onto the interstate, the after-work traffic congestion had cleared and he had pressed the accelerator a little more. "Cameron, please be okay," said Gerard out loud. "I'm so sorry. I promised that I wouldn't let anyone hurt you again, and I let him take you," he thought as he drove faster. "I'm coming." Gerard was almost at the east side of the city when he picked up his car phone and dialed his house.

"Dr. Wright where are you?" Detective Fisher answered after the first ring. "We've got men out right now looking for you."

"I'm on my way to the north shore. That's where Cameron is. He's with a man named David Boudreau."

"David Boudreau, are you—do you mean *the* David Boudreau on the billboards who is running for office?" Fisher did not sound convinced..

"Yes, I've talked to someone who saw him with Cameron and they followed as far as the bridge." Gerard could tell he wasn't getting through. "It's him. I know it."

"You said that about Alan Sullivan too, Dr. Wright. The best thing for you to do is come back right now and let us handle it. Even if you are right, you can't…"

"I'm on my way to his cabin now."

"All right, what's the address?" asked Fisher.

"I'm not sure. I haven't been here in a couple of years, but I think I can find my way back."

"I'll alert the sheriff's office over there. We'll have the address in a couple of minutes. We're on our way, but listen Dr. Wright, don't try to tackle him by yourself. Wait for us, and we'll get the boy back safely."

"Okay," said Gerard though he knew that he was not going to wait. He thought about the gun in his glove compartment. "But hurry."

"Damn that crazy old man," said David as he leaned against a tree and put a hand over his bloody arm. "Why can't he mind his own business?" he hissed and tried to peer over his shoulder towards the truck. No more shots were fired. David hoped that he was dead. As soon as he finished with the kid, he would dispose of the old man. This was getting out of control. The shots would go unnoticed, he thought, there was always someone showing off their guns near this lake. "How the hell am I going to explain all this?"

He kept walking in the direction that he had seen Cameron go. "It's no use. You know you can't get away from me." He ignored his pain and kept moving. A few yards ahead of him, beside a tree, sat the boy. David walked faster, wondering why he had stopped running. When he reached for him, he saw that he was having some kind of seizure. This would make it easier. He knew that he would not try to fight him when he picked him up and carried him to the edge of the lake at the back of the property.

The water looked black in the darkness. Only the light of the crescent moon illuminated his steps. Cameron was unconscious and barely breathing. David did not have time to wait for him to die. He would drown him, then row out, weigh the body down and sink it to the bottom. The whole mess would be over and Cameron de la Valle would be just another missing child. There were hundreds of them every week. David got down on his knees at the edge of the lake and placed Cameron in the water. He held onto him with one arm so that he wouldn't float out and wake up. He might be able to swim, for all he knew. The whole world seemed to go silent for the next few seconds.

He was startled when Cameron woke up and began to struggle to free himself. When they had the house built they had new steps down to the water put in to make it more comfortable for Susan and the kids to get down to the sailboat. Cameron tried to hold on to the base of the steps now, to keep David from pushing him under.

"I told you that I would be back for you later, and here I am," he said as he held the child underwater easily, even with one arm. Suddenly, he felt an excruciating pain on the back of his head, and then he felt nothing.

Gerard dropped the piece of firewood that he had used to hit David and looked at the black water for Cameron. He was terrified momentarily when he did not see him, and immediately dropped down into the water to look for him. He did not have to look though; Cameron was underwater right at the base of the steps and Gerard lifted him out and laid him on the deck.

"Cameron! Cameron!" Gerard looked at his gray, lifeless body. "Oh please God, no," he whispered, then without hesitation tilted Cameron's head back and began to administer a short resuscitative breath into his mouth. He counted to three and tried again, but still nothing.

Gerard counted again and breathed into him. He was about to give in to the flood of panic he was fighting inside, when he heard Cameron cough and breathe. He picked him up and started towards the house with him. He was breathing, but unconscious. He was a few footsteps away from the French doors, when he heard the bullet go past his ear.

"I can't let you leave."

Gerard, still holding Cameron in his arms, turned around to face David. "You'll have to kill me first. I think you've already had some experience with that. I saw your caretaker out front too."

"I never meant for it to go this far."

"Why, David?" Gerard's heart was pounding as he looked at the gun barrel.

"I had to do it. Why couldn't you stay out of it? I didn't know you were going to get involved. It was the drugs that made me do it."

"You think I have sympathy for you?" Gerard yelled back. "I know what you did to this child. I've been reading Leon's diary."

"His what?" David's face contorted even more. "No! That can't be true!" He cried for a few seconds and then it turned to hysterical laughter. "It figures he would write things down. Then you know about us?"

Gerard nodded.

"Well, did you know that the bastard was going to ruin me? I went over there that night to try to talk to him and he laughed at me. I saw the kid run and hide, but I wasn't planning on stabbing him. I had always given him everything he wanted and after everything I'd done for him, he was going to tell everyone about us. All because of that damned kid. He found me with him that night. I thought he had passed out. I couldn't help myself. He actually got angry and tried to fight me before he left here. He dropped him off at a church, like I was evil. He thought he was the only one who could touch the boy." He started to laugh again.

Gerard could have killed him with his bare hands then. He had never felt this kind of disgust before. "This won't end here. I'll tell everyone I know. I'll go to the papers. You know if you kill me, I won't be just another missing child."

Gerard saw David's finger move, but he couldn't react before the bullet struck him in the shoulder. He fell back against the French doors, breaking them and landing on David's den floor. He was still holding Cameron, but quickly pushed him away. Gerard reached into his jacket pocket and took out his own gun. David was coming towards him with his finger still on the trigger when Gerard fired three times. David fell to the ground. Gerard could see his eyes, lifeless, staring up at the sky.

Gerard crawled over to the phone to dial 911, when he saw the blue lights flashing outside the house. He reached for Cameron and pulled him into his arms. His body was soaking wet and cold. His eyes were still closed. "It's over now. I'm so sorry. I love you." He felt tears streaming down his face as the police and paramedics rushed into the room.

Epilogue

Eight days later, Gerard and Cameron were released from the hospital. Gerard's gunshot wound still caused him pain in his shoulder, but he had always been a fast healer. Against his doctor's orders, he had spent the majority of the week at Cameron's bedside, talking to him and praying for him to awake from his coma. When Gerard awakened from his own nap on the fourth evening, he found Cameron's emerald green eyes looking back at him.

After signing a stack of paperwork, Gerard waited to be wheeled out.

"Why do I have to have this stupid wheelchair? I feel fine."

"It's regulation," said Henry, the nurse who had been taking care of Gerard all week.

"This is fun Gerry," Cameron said. He was grinning as the pediatric nurse wheeled him into the room.

Gerard stopped frowning and started to smile. "I suppose I'll make the best of it. Come on, let's get out of here."

When they got back to Gerard's mansion, a lovely young woman was standing on the front porch.

"Well hello, Alma." Gerard winced a little when she gave him and Cameron a hug.

"I've been calling the hospital, but they wouldn't tell me anything. I came by to see you two, but they told me you went home this morning. I just got here" She reached out and touched Cameron's face.

"Hi." Cameron looked up at her.

"That's wonderful." She looked at Gerard. "I was hoping to talk to you."

"Now is fine. Let me get these bags."

"No, let me help you." Alma picked up the overnight bags. "What I was wondering," she asked as they walked inside, "was if you needed a secretary or something?"

Gerard sat down on the sofa and Cameron sat down beside him.

"I didn't want that money. I let Luis keep it. He's gone to Miami. I need a job now though." She gave a half-hearted smile.

"I don't need a secretary," he said. He glanced at Cameron and saw the disappointed cross his face. "But we do need a nanny, preferably one who could live in." Gerard could tell from their smiles that the idea appealed to both Alma and Cameron. "Good, then it's settled." Gerard stood up just as the phone rang.

"I'll get it." Cameron picked up the phone before Gerard could stop him. He handed the phone to Gerard. "It's the recording from Mama."

Gerard accepted the call. "Magdalene, how are you?"

"I'm okay. I didn't get to call Cameron yesterday. Is he…"

"He's fine. I'll let you talk to him. I've given a statement to the DA's office and gotten you a new lawyer. We're going to get you a new trial. I don't know how long the process will be, but try to be patient."

"I'm going to be okay now. My baby is safe. I don't know if I thanked you for saving my son's life."

"No thanks are required." Gerard smiled down at Cameron. "Here, I'll let you talk to him."

The 13-story parking garage of the tallest office building in New Orleans was particularly deserted that Saturday after New Year's. The black Jaguar pulled in and parked on the fifth floor next to the silver SUV with the tinted windows.

"Well, it looks like you picked a good place to meet." Rob got into the Jaguar.

"I guess you've been reading the newspaper."

"Yeah, David did not have everything under control the way he said he did."

"I am sure he did not count on Gerard Wright turning into a hero. David was so vain that he could never have lived through all this negative publicity. Did you know about him and Leon?"

"No, I didn't. I thought it was just business. When you told him to get rid of Leon, I didn't know he'd have personal reasons to want him dead, too."

"There certainly wasn't any love lost between you and your cousin was there? Anyway, David should have taken care of him and the kid that night. That was what we agreed on."

"What now?"

"Well, it will look too obvious if the kid has an accident now. The papers said that they expect he'll make a complete recovery. The little prodigy will probably be playing another concert inside of a month. Besides, too many people are looking into David's life right now. I don't want them uncovering us."

"But Cameron would be easy to…"

"No, we've had enough trouble for now. We'll have to slow the business down for now. Later, when things have died down, the boy will die—something simple this time. David made things way too complicated. Then we can get back to business."

"I still can't believe David was so careless as to let Leon in on our entire operation, and with the kid around."

"Leon won't be telling anyone about us, and Cameron will be joining him soon."

THE END

Printed in the United States
18876LVS00002B/3